PIGS' MEAT
Selected Writings of Thomas Spence

Pigs' Meat

The Selected Writings of Thomas Spence, Radical and Pioneer Land Reformer

With an introductory essay and notes by G.I. Gallop

Spokesman

First published in 1982 by:
Spokesman
Bertrand Russell House
Gamble Street
Nottingham

Cloth ISBN 0 85124 315 0

Copyright © G.I. Gallop and Spokesman

This book is copyright under the Berne Convention. All rights are reserved. Apart from any fair dealings for the purpose of private study, research, criticism or review, as permitted under the Copyright Act, 1956, no part of this published may be reproduced stored in a retrieval system, or transmitted, in any form or by any means, electronic, electrical, chemical, mechanical, optical, photocopying, recording or otherwise, without the prior permission of the copyright owner. Enquiries should be addressed to the publishers.

British Library Cataloguing in Publication Data

Spence, Thomas
Thomas Spence — (Socialist classics; no.2)
1. Socialism
2. Labor and laboring classes — Great Britain — History
I. Title II. Gallop, G.I. III. Series
335'.1092'4 HD8393.S/
ISBN 0 85124 315 0

Printed by the Russell Press Ltd., Nottingham

"Mail coaches were now [1819] general, and in these I usually travelled on my journeys from Scotland to and from London. On one of these journeys, about this period, I was travelling from London to the North, and was the only inside passenger in the coach when it arrived at Newark, where both horses were changed; and while this process was going on, both doors of the mail coach were at the same time opened, and a gentleman came in on each side, and they commenced a conversation together . . . Their conversation continued for some time, when one said something to my supposed intelligent companion, who was opposite to me, which induced him to say — 'Why that is Owenism! Who would ever think of anything so absurd?' At this I opened my ears, and I heard this subject canvassed between them, and I soon found that the intelligent opponent knew little of Owenism, as he called the notions which he had received of it.

I then said to him — 'Pray what is this Owenism about which you are conversing?' My intelligent companion very readily replied, stating the usual mistakes given to the public by those who thought they had an interest in opposing my views, or who had not sufficient capacity to comprehend them . . .

When he concluded, I said — 'I must be quite in error upon this subject, for my ideas of it are very different from those you have just stated'. 'Then', he said, 'will you have the kindness to explain your views of it?' I said, 'Willingly', and I entered fully into the principles and practices, and these we discussed with animation and interest for nearly three hours, when at last he said I am sure you are Spence, (the advocate of that time of an equal division of the land,) or else Owen."

The Life of Robert Owen, Written by Himself (London, 1857), Vol.I, p.227.

Acknowledgements

My thanks to William Thomas, Terry Parssinen and Leslie Macfarlane who read and commented on earlier drafts of the Introductory Essay.

G.I. Gallop

Contents

Acknowledgements	6
Part I. Introductory Essay: Thomas Spence and the Real Rights of Man by G.I. Gallop	9
Introduction	11
The Man and his Life	14
The Ethical Foundations: Liberty, Community and the Rights of Man	20
The Structure and Functioning of Spensonia	28
The Transition	41
Conclusion	50
Part II. Selected Writings	55
Introductory Notes	57
The Rights of Man (1793)	59
An Interesting Conversation, between a Gentleman and the Author, on the Subject of the foregoing Lecture	67
The Marine Republic (1794)	77
A Further Account of Spensonia (1794)	80
The End of Oppression (1795)	91
Hawk! how the Trumpet's Sound . . .	98
A Letter from Ralph Hodge, to his cousin Thomas Bull (1795)	100
The National Debt	105
The Meridian Sun of Liberty (1796)	107
The Rights of Infants (1797)	111
The Restorer of Society to its Natural State (1803)	127
The Constitution of Spensonia (1803)	166
Part III. Bibliography of Thomas Spence	187

I
Introductory Essay: Thomas Spence and the Real Rights of Man
by G. I. Gallop

Introduction

The story of the emergence of British radicalism and socialism in the late eighteenth and early nineteenth centuries needs careful attention.[1] For too long accounts have concentrated "upon one dramatic episode — *the* Revolution — to which all that goes before and after must be related".[2] Thus we are told by Harold Laski that before the influence of the French Revolution there was no sense of the existence of a social problem in the radical movement that developed after 1760. The early radicals were concerned with "political forms" rather than "social substance".[3] It has also become commonplace to argue that British socialism did not take shape until *after* 1815, Robert Owen's influence being placed at the centre of the picture. The social critics of the 1790s took the radical case to the threshold of socialism but did not cross it. For those who argue this way the Industrial Revolution is decisive:

> "So far as Britain is concerned, socialist thinking properly so called made its appearance in the 1820s, when an urban factory proletariat had begun to form . . .
> A socialist doctrine could not be formulated until industrial capitalism had unveiled its secret, and even then the bulk of the British labour movement remained wedded for many years to the non-socialist radicalism of an earlier day."[4]

However, like all "ideal-type" conceptions of intellectual history this one needs to be significantly qualified. It is an over-simplified account of a more complex reality. The belief that the French Revolution was decisive in the development of social-radicalism, the assumption that the eighteenth-century social formation did not allow for a socialist critique and the centrality given to Robert Owen all need to be questioned.[5] In such a process of re-writing a study of Thomas Spence (1750 to 1814) is more than useful. Sometime netmaker, clerk, schoolteacher, bookseller, saloop seller and dealer in token coins Spence had largely developed his views on property and politics before he shifted from Newcastle to London in 1792.[6]

By combining together contemporary natural rights doctrines[7] with the communitarianism of the radically-inclined dissenting sects[8] and certain aspects of republican thought kept alive in the eighteenth-century,[9] Spence was able to produce a comprehensive argument for political and social revolution based on what he liked to call the "real" rights of man. Like Winstanley and the Diggers, Spence and his followers took radical ideology into the world of socialism. Indeed, he was the first to argue unambiguously for democratic republicanism, common ownership and popular revolution and is testimony to the fact that social-radicalism in this period was not a derivative of the French Revolution. Nor is a study of Spence simply "an interesting study in British Socialist origins"[10] as he played some part, albeit a small one, in influencing the theory and thereby the practice of sections of the radical and working-class movements. The Spenceans were particularly active in the revolutionary agitation of the post-war years up to and including the Cato Street Conspiracy. From that point on they no longer existed as a group but simply as a tendency of opinion within the wider movement.[11]

Footnotes

1. On the relationship between "radicalism" and "socialism" see G.D.H. Cole, "British Radicals and the Socialist Tradition", *Phoenix Quarterly,* Autumn 1946, pp.5-9 and Willard Wolfe *From Radicalism to Socialism: Men and Ideas in the Formation of Fabian Socialist Doctrines 1881-1889* (New Haven and London, 1975), ch.1.
2. E.P. Thompson, "The Peculiarities of the English", in *The Poverty of Theory and other Essays* (London, 1978), p.47. Although relevant in another context Thompson's quote is ideal for my purposes. Hopefully, however, I am in "the spirit" of Thompson's enquiry.

3. *The Rise of European Liberalism* (London, 1936), p.205.
4. G. Lichtheim, *The Origins of Socialism* (London, 1968), pp.102, 104.
5. For too long, as Iorweth Prothero has argued in a very important article, the reference to Owen has too often been a substitute for explanation when looking at the movements of the 1820s and 30s: "It is surely time that 'Owenism', an amorphous term if not defined, is cut down to size, and it should not be necessary to insist that the different aspects of Owenism must be related to persistent strands in working-class activity — artisan self-employment, anti-Christian propaganda, Spenceanism and land reform"; "William Benbow and the concept of the 'General Strike'," *Past and Present*, No.63 (1974), p.155.
6. For the only book-length study of Spence, now somewhat dated see Olive D. Rudkin, *Thomas Spence and his Connections* (London, 1927). There is also an unpublished thesis: T.M. Parssinen, *Thomas Spence and the Spenceans: A Study of Revolutionary Utopianism in the England of George III* (Brandeis Univ., PhD, 1968). See also Francis Place, "Memoir of Spence", *Place Papers*, British Museum Add. MSS 27808, ff.151-224; P.M. Kemp-Ashraf, "Thomas Spence", in P.M. Kemp-Ashraf and Jack Mitchell (eds), *Essays in Honour of William Gallacher* (Berlin, 1966), pp.271-291; T.M. Parssinen, "Thomas Spence and the Origins of English Land Nationalization", *Journal of the History of Ideas*, 34 (1973), pp.135-141; and Thomas R. Knox, "Thomas Spence: The Trumpet of Jubilee", *Past and Present*, No.76 (1977), pp.75-98. There are two collections of Spence's writings, neither of which is comprehensive: A.W. Waters (ed.), *Spence and his Political Works* (Leamington Spa, 1917) and Kemp-Ashraf and Mitchell, *William Gallacher*, supplement.
7. See H. T. Dickinson, "The Rights of Man: From John Locke to Tom Paine", in O.D. Edwards and G.A. Shepperson (eds.), *Scotland, Europe and the American Revolution* (Edinburgh, 1976), pp.38-48.
8. See W.H.G. Armytage, *Heavens Below: Utopian Experiments in England 1560-1960* (London, 1961), chs.1-3 and E.P. Thompson, *The making of the English Working Class* (2nd ed., Harmondsworth, 1968), ch 2.
9. Caroline Robbins, *The Eighteenth Century Commonwealthman* ... (Cambridge Mass., 1959) and J.G.A. Pocock, *Politics, Language and Time* (London, 1972), ch.4.
10. G.D.H. Cole, *Socialist Thought: The Forerunners 1789-1850* (London, 1953), p.25.
11. It was not until the land reform agitation of the late nineteenth-century that Spence was rediscovered as a "precursor". See H.M. Hyndman, *Nationalization of Land in 1775 and 1882* (London, 1882).

The Man and his Life[1]

Spence was born in 1750, of Scottish parents, in Newcastle-upon-Tyne. His father was a netmaker by trade and kept a small hardware store. Spence's mother, a native of the Orkneys, also kept a small store, for the sale of stockings. By Spence's own account they were hard-working but poor, a contrast he pointed to later in his life to explain the origin of his desire to change the world.

The Spence family was deeply religious, Thomas' father teaching him to read the Bible and reflect upon what he was reading as he progressed. In 1764 the dissenting congregation to which the Spences belonged[2] summoned to Newcastle the Rev. James Murray. Murray was a graduate of the University of Edinburgh who had been dismissed from a post in Alnwick for his belief that each congregation should have the right to adopt their own modes of government. He was a political as well as a theological radical and became a friend and mentor to the young Thomas.[3]

Although Spence learnt his father's trade he soon became a clerk with a local smith. Before long, however, he had opened his own school and was teaching in other schools in Newcastle. He developed a phonetic alphabet which he hoped would help break down class barriers by teaching correct pronunciation to everyone.[4] "Why", he asked, "should People be laughed at all their Lives for betraying their vulgar Education when the Evil is so easily remedied".[5] To publicise his alphabet he had many of his tracts published in phonetic form.

When men of "learning and substance" formed the Newcastle Philosophical Society Spence was invited to join and read a paper outlining his views. This he did in 1775.[6] To protect and foster the rights of man, he argued, it was necessary for the inhabitants of each Parish to meet together and form themselves into a Corporation which would become the sole owner of the land and its appurtenances. The land would then be leased for a rent varying with its quantity and quality. The rent would go to the Parish Corporation and be used to finance services and meet the expenses of a National Government needed to deal with inter-parish disputes and defence. Soon after Spence was expelled from the Society not, apparently, for his views but because he hawked the lecture on the streets of Newcastle.

Undeterred Spence set up his own debating society and published a few tracts further outlining his views. Unfortunately for Spence, however, he met with little success. He lost his job at the local school and children were kept away from his school. On top of political and economic difficulties he entered into an unsuccessful marriage in 1781. His increasing isolation, exacerbated by the death of Murray in 1782 and his publisher, Thomas Saint, in 1788, left him irritable and restless: "He was often heard to say that there was no scope for ability in a provincial town, and that London was the only place where a man of talent could display his powers".[7]

From 1792 London was his home. He made a living in a variety of ways — from a shop and later a mobile stall he sold tracts and pamphlets, saloop (a drink made from sassafras) and token coins, some of which he had struck for himself.[8] However, in none of his commercial ventures did he meet with any success and he remained very poor for the rest of his life. Nor did he win a significant following for his ideas. This failure, however, was not due to any lack of effort as Spence was a constant source of handbills, placards, broadsheets, chalk and charcoal notices and tracts and pamphlets on various aspects of what he liked to call his "Plan". William Hone, in a letter to Place, described him at work:

"His 'vehicle' ... was very like a baker's close barrow, the pamphlets were exhibited outside, and when he sold one he took it from within, and handed and recommended others with strong expressions of hate to the powers that were, and prophecies of what should happen to the whole race of 'Landlords'."[9]

After his first wife died in Newcastle, she having stayed behind and kept a store, Spence married again. He proposed to a young girl who took his fancy one day. She consented, wanting to punish her first lover after a recent rebuff. Soon after she deserted Spence and left with a sea-captain for the West Indies. She eventually returned to Spence who forgave her but soon asked her to leave. However, Spence won the admiration of his friends by paying his wife 8/- a week for the rest of her life. Subsequently Spence was to advocate easy divorce: "It is enough to make one shudder to think of being indissolubly bound to a Spendthrift, a Drunkard, a Sluggard, a Tyrant, a Brute, a Trollop, a Vixen..."[10]

Twice Spence issued his own penny periodical: *Pigs' Meat; or Lessons for the Swinish Multitude* (1793-1795) and *Giant-Killer; or Anti-Landlord* (1814). In them he printed articles, songs and poems of his own plus extracts from other writers. The single writer most quoted was James Harrington; More, Milton, Locke, Sidney, Fletcher, Trenchard, Swift, Price and Barlow also appeared frequently. It is worth noticing with Caroline Robbins that "the exponent of a new egalitarianism looked not to levelling tracts, but to the great Whig canon for support".[11] By taking the natural rights doctrine literally and infusing it with social and communitarian content Spence took the "Real Whig" tradition into the world of socialism.

Spence was arrested and detained on numerous occasions. He was gaoled three times — once in 1794, for seven months under the suspension of Habeus Corpus, again in 1798 under the suspension of Habeus Corpus, and finally for twelve months in 1801 after being found guilty of sedition. The government of the day was convinced that Spence was involved in treasonable activity (as opposed to general incitement) but was never able to produce any real evidence. In 1794 Spence was arrested, the intention being to charge him with High Treason. It was alleged that there was drilling associated with his shop. However, when the charges against Thomas Hardy, Horne Tooke and John Thelwall fell,[12] the government decided not to proceed against Spence.

According to Place Spence was a very small and unappealing man with a thin and wrinkled face coupled with a large and uneven mouth. He spoke with a northern accent and had a slight speech impediment. Because of his poverty he was generally dressed in old and sometimes ragged clothes. Like Thomas Bewick[13] (who knew Spence in his Newcastle days), Place also spoke of his contempt for those who disagreed with him, his words and manner expressing this contempt. He simply could not believe that such people were honest. It is not surprising, then, that Place should conclude that "he had not, therefore, many points of attraction".[14] Nevertheless, like Bewick, he seemed to admire Spence for his sincerity and commitment in the face of government harassment and personal poverty.

Given his belief that his Plan could not be compromised Spence was bound to become a relatively lone figure in the London radical movement. He wanted converts not colleagues. Still, by 1807 at least, a Spencean Society had been formed and met to debate questions, discuss Spence's Plan and sell his pamphlets. The meeting would end with song, jest and drink. Thomas Evans,[15] one-time secretary of the London Corresponding Society and member of the shadowy United Englishmen in the late 1790s, turned most of his energies to the Spencean cause after his release from gaol in 1801. Evans was also the key figure in the formation of the Society of Spencean Philanthropists after Spence's death in 1814. It was organised in divisions along the lines of the LCS.[16] Also attached to Spenceanism before 1815 were Allen Davenport[17] who kept alive Spence's ideas in the 1830s and several ultra-revolutionaries of the post-1815 period – Arthur Thistlewood,[18] Thomas Preston,[19] and James Watson.[20] It is not clear whether they joined just before or after Spence died.

Whatever his views on the transition then – to be outlined in Chapter IV – there is no evidence that Spence was actually engaged in preparing (except in the most general sense) for a revolution.[21] Nor was he integrated into the mainstream of metropolitan radicalism. He despised the *political* radicals and social and economic *reformers* for being politically naive and intellectually incoherent. He rejected any form of politics based on a distinction between minimum and maximum demands.

Only three numbers of Spence's new periodical *Giant-Killer* had appeared when he died in September 1814. About forty friends attended his funeral, "a pair of scales draped in white ribbons and with an equal quantity of earth in each balance, to symbolise the innocence and the justice of his views, preceded his corpse"[22] to the burial ground of St. James's, Hampstead Road.

Footnotes

1. Except where stated biographical detail is from Rudkin, *Thomas Spence* and T.M. Parssinen, "Thomas Spence" in Joseph O. Baylen and Norbet J. Gossman (eds.), *Biographical Dictionary of Modern British Radicals Volume 1: 1770-1830* (Sussex, 1979), pp.454-458. Hereafter referred to as *B.D.M.B.R.*
2. One of Spence's brothers, Jeremiah, joined the local Glassite community. Founded by John Glas who had been expelled from the Church of Scotland in 1728 they believed in a complete republican equality in their own communities. See Eneas Mackenzie, *A Descriptive and Historical Account of the Town and County of Newcastle* (2 vols; Newcastle, 1827), I, pp. 399-401.
3. See "Biographical Sketch of Rev. James Murray" in a collection of Murray's sermons published by William Hone in 1819: *Sermons to Asses* (London, 1819).
4. *The Real Reading Made Easy* . . . (Newcastle, 1782).
5. *Giant-Killer,* No.1, p.2.
6. The original edition of the lecture is not extant. The first edition available was published in London in 1793 (4th ed.). It has been reprinted in Max Beer (ed.), *The Pioneers of Land Reform* (London, 1920), pp.5-16. Future references to the *Lecture* will be from this source.
7. "Memoir of Spence", *Newcastle Magazine,* No.3, January 1821, in Add. MSS 27808, f.304.
8. See Waters, *Spence and his Political Works,* introduction and C. Brunel and P.M. Jackson, "Tokens as a source of labour and radical history", *Bulletin of the Society for the Study of Labour History,* No.13 (Autumn 1966), pp.26-36.
9. "Hone to Place", Add. MSS 27808, f.314.
10. *The Restorer of Society to its Natural State* (London, 1801) reprinted in Waters, *Spence,* p.46. Future references to the *Restorer* will be from this source.

11. Robbins, *Commonwealthman*, p.322. It seems more than likely that Murray, educated at Edinburgh in the late 1750s, introduced Spence to the Real Whig literature. On Scotland and Real Whiggery see *ibid.*, Ch.6.
12. See Albert Goodwin, *The Friends of Liberty: The English Democratic Movement in the Age of the French Revolution* (London, 1979), Ch.9.
13. Iain Bain (ed.), *Memoir of Thomas Bewick Written by Himself* (London, 1975), pp.52-53.
14. Add. MSS 27808, ff.152-154.
15. See *B.D.M.B.R.*, I, pp.164-166. Evans was the author of two Spencean tracts; *Christian Policy, the Salvation of Empire* (London, 1816) and *Christian Policy in full Practice among the People of Harmony* . . . (London, 1818).
16. On Spencean politics after 1815 see T.M. Parssinen, "The revolutionary party in London, 1816-1821", *Bulletin of the Institute of Historical Research*, 45 (1972), pp.266-282.
17. See *B.D.M.B.R.*, I, pp.111-113. He was the author of *The Life, Writings and Principles of Thomas Spence* (London, 1836).
18. See *B.D.M.B.R.*, I, pp.471-475.
19. *Ibid.*, pp.389-391.
20. *Ibid.*, pp.512-514.
21. This contrasts with the post-war years. However, as they became more conspiratorial they became less concerned with Spencean ideology. Evans, on the other hand, was less inclined to action and was not implicated in any of the attempts at insurrection. He was mainly concerned with the propagation of Spencean principles. See Parssinen, "Revolutionary Party".
22. Rudkin, *Thomas Spence*, p.142.

The Ethical Foundations: Liberty, Community and the Rights of Man

Spence's ethics were informed by a particular interpretation of the scriptures and nourished by the radical doctrine of man's natural and inalienable rights to life, liberty and property. Mixed in as well were specifically republican ideas which had been kept alive in the eighteenth-century by the so-called "Commonwealthmen".[1]

It was initially Spence's father who introduced him to the *Bible*. Spence made much of the Levetical Jubilee when God would intervene in human history and restore men to their original, and rightful, possessions.[2] In such a state the land was held in common. James Murray reinforced this interpretation. For him the *Bible* was a charter of rights and liberties. He attacked the unjust taxation of the poor, the corruption in political life and the so-called "agricultural improvement" which he saw increasing the numbers of idle and lazy at the expense of the industrious. *"The claims of freedom and liberty"*, he wrote, *"ended with the division of the common"*.[3]

Underneath all of Spence's arguments was the picture of society as a great machine which, if placed on the right foundations, would be impossible to shift. In such a conception the "whole" was greater than the "parts":

> . . . when the public machine is thus set a going on nature's principles, like nature itself, it will never err to any great degree, but on the least aberration immediately rebound to its just equilibrium.[4]

It was necessary to get the principles right and then to find the correct "fit" between those principles and the political, social and economic institutions of a nation.

Quite explicitly Spence saw himself as a spokesman for the common people. When speaking of them he referred either to the poor and disinherited in general[5] or to the labouring poor in particular.[6] Thus at his trial in 1801 he complained about the class-bias in his jury. For the trial to be fair, he claimed, at least half the jury should be labourers.[7] Lined up against the labourers were "the landlords and stockholders who subsist on revenues extorted legally as they say, from the rest of mankind" as well as their allies and dependents — placemen and pensioners, lawyers and attorneys, servants, soldiers and sailors.[8] The civilisation they ruled, he maintained, was founded upon conquest and violence. By creating a system based on the private ownership of the land they were able to systematically exploit the labouring class. From both the point of view of production and consumption the labourers were vital:

> ". . . the farmer could neither proceed without labourers nor find purchases for his corn and cattle. It would be just the same with the building landlord, for he could neither procure workmen to build, nor tenants to pay him rent."[9]

However, because of the ownership system the great mass of the people did not receive any of the benefits of the increased output for which they were responsible. On the contrary "in proportion as the comforts of life increased by Man's labour and Ingenuity, so did the rapacity of men also increase to rob each other".[10]

In his many writings he either mentioned explicitly, or implicitly through the concrete proposals he put forward, a whole plethora of human rights. In his *Constitution of Spensonia* (London, 1801) he began:

> 1. The end of Society is common happiness. Government is instituted to secure to man the enjoyment of his natural and imprescriptible rights.
> 2. These rights are Equality, Liberty, Safety, and Property, natural and acquired.[11]

At the centre of his commitments was a belief in liberty — of religion, thought, expression, assembly and, importantly, movement within and between countries. The laws should be "few, explicit, and the same in every Parish, being made by the common Legislature".[12] At the same time economic activity and relationships should be free; no kind of labour, culture or commerce being forbidden to the industrious citizen[13] and the ports "open and free to Nations and Foreigners without custom house, or Officers to molest them".[14] To engage in economic activity rent on the land used had to be paid to the community; this was the only condition:

> "Freedom to do anything whatever cannot there be bought; a thing is either entirely prohibited, as theft or murder; or entirely free to everyone without tax or price, and the rents are still not so high, notwithstanding all that is done with them, as they were formerly for only the maintenance of a few haughty, unthankful landlords."[15]

On top of these rights to freedom, and essential to their preservation, "every citizen has an equal right of concurring in the formation of the law and in the nomination of his mandatores or agents".[16] Those belonging to the female sex, he added, should have "the same right of suffrage in their respective parishes as the Men".[17] He threw scorn at those "aristocrats" who pictured government as a mysterious process which only a few could understand and participate in. The time would come, he explained, when "we are not mere spectators in the world, but as all men ought to be, actors".[18] Thus in a society run on Spencean principles the law would be "the free and solemn expression of the general will".[19]

In writing of rights to property Spence made a distinction between "land" and "moveable property". To the former everyone had an equal and inalienable right. By it he meant " *the land with all its appurtenances, as structures, buildings, and fixtures, and mines, woods, waters etc., contained within itself*".[20] Such land would all be taken into common ownership and let, the rent varying not only with the quantity but also with the quality of the land. Moveable property on the other hand — money, plate, jewellery, furniture, apparel, and cattle — would not be subject to common ownership. Therefore, once everyone's right to the land was established, a degree of accumulation of moveable property was possible but unimportant because "when wealth cannot be rooted and fixed in land, it is of a fluctuating and evaporating nature, and is apt, like the moisture of the earth to take wings and fly away, unless restored by the showers of industry".[21]

In his original presentation of his ideas Spence argued that a man's right to equal portions of the land and its productions was founded upon his right to life because "the land or earth ... with everything in or on the same, or pertaining thereto is the means of life itself".[22] However, it becomes clearer in his later writings that the right to and equal share of the land is seen first and foremost as a means to give everyone access to productive capital which they can work for themselves. Independent, productive labour unmediated by relations between employer and employee was seen as an end-in-itself. As far as was possible, he wrote to Charles Hall in 1807, it was necessary to reduce the number of labourers and journeymen in any line of business. In "Spensonia" all "would be little farmers and little Mastermen".[23] He also made it clear that relations between employer and employee, where they still existed, would be radically transformed:

> "Every man may engage his services and his time, but he cannot sell himself; his person is not alienable property. The law does not acknowledge servitude; there can exist only an engagement of care and gratitude between the man who labours and the man who employs him."[24]

However, he did not give up his commitment to welfare (the right of all to the means of subsistence). This was to be guaranteed by a surplus rent policy in which the surplus left over after the expenses of government had been met would be shared equally amongst all the inhabitants — men and women, young and old, rich and poor, legitimate and illegitimate. This would guarantee a reasonable standard of life for all, the payment being made every quarter. Spence liked to compare each of his Parishes with fraternal or benefit societies caring for all their members.[25] Given that the rent would vary with the quality as well as the quantity of the land let, any improvements made would, in part, be passed on to the community at large. In justifying this redistribution Spence introduced the idea of the *social* nature of work:

> "Slaves and unfortunate Men have cultivated the Earth, adorned it with buildings and filled it with all kinds of Riches. And the Wealth which enabled you to set these People to work, was got by Hook or Crook from Society. Pray, was ever a solitary Savage found to be rich? No – all Riches come from Society, I mean the Labouring Part of it. And when these improvements return back to Society, they will only return to the Source from whence they came."[26]

Nowhere else does Spence mention or develop this conception of labour.

Interestingly enough it was the productive rather than the welfare side of his ethic which was seen to be the most important. "It is", he wrote (as a citizen of "Spensonia"), "the security of property, exempt from wars, the freedom from taxes, from revenue officers, from oaths, informers and every irksome shackle, that constitutes our supreme happiness".[27] His was a utopia of small producers and cheap government. By removing the superstructure of landlordism and corruption from the backs of the people they could enjoy the full fruits of their labour, subject only to the conditions (1) that they have only a fair share of the land and (2) that they contribute to the common good through the payment of rent. In this way the correct balance between freedom, incentives and equality would be found.

Implicit in all of Spence's writings was also the idea that every citizen had a right to the best that could be offered in modern economic conditions. He abused those "idle aristocrats" who preached "temperance, labour, patience and submission".[28] Regular holidays and festivals were necessary to provide relief from toil:

> "Even the Popes ordained Holidays in abundance and Times of Feastings, and giving Gifts and making merry; nay, their Monasteries with all their faults were often Blessings and Asylums for the Distrest both in body and mind."[29]

Secondly, each Parish would provide social, cultural and educational facilities for all its citizens. There should also be a National University where every Parish could send one of its most promising youths; the person to be chosen by secret ballot.[30] Finally, the pattern of consumption would be characterised not only by a greater degree of equality than in the present world but also by that quantity and quality of goods necessary to satisfy both "natural" and "artificial" wants. Indeed the existence of universal education would spread the demand for refinements and luxuries.[31] In 1782 he described "Spensonia" (then called "Crusonia") in the following terms:

> "It is full of superb and well furnished Shops and has every Appearance of Grandeur, Opulence, and Convenience, one can conceive to be in a large Place, flourishing with Trade and Manufactures."[32]

"Would you", he asked Charles Hall, "have us all to become again Goths and Vandals and give up every elegant comfort of life?"[33]

Nevertheless there does appear to be some tension in his thought on the question of consumption, trade and manufacturing. In 1801 he spoke of there being too many artificers and tradesmen; measures needed to be taken to get people back to the land.[34] In "A Dream" he actually proposed the returning of everyone to "the natural occupation of Tillage, until the whole Earth be as the Garden of Eden".[35] Here the right to land is described in terms of *the right to an agricultural form of employment.* Would not this imply a qualification of the case for an expansion in the amount and range of consumption? For Spence it seems to be a question of balance. In "Spensonia", he said, "men would learn to moderate their desires, and cease to aspire after boundless wealth, which they could have no means of consolidating".[36] Given that freedom of movement and the market still existed the right balance between agriculture, trade and manufacturing would automatically be found:

> "Trade will be genuine, unforced and natural. For none will be in Trade and Manufactures, but those who can live well by them, because, Tillage would be open to all in the Case of Difficulty."[37]

Through this eclectic mixture of freedom and equality Spence believed the truly fraternal society would emerge. Suppress any of the elements and the laws of nature would not be realised. Thus the stress he placed on the *plurality* of elements which he believed made up the human condition — freedom and order, equality and inequality, work and play.

Should the balance between them be upset then the Millenium would not be a reality. The key problem, however, was to get the correct fit between these ideals and the political, social and economic institutions and practices.

Footnotes

1. For example the idea of an agrarian law to redistribute property and underpin the "republic" was advocated by certain radicals. See Robbins, *Commonwealthman* and H.T. Dickinson, *Liberty and Property: Political Ideology in Eighteenth-Century Britain* (London, 1977), Ch.6.
2. Spence reprinted Leveticus, Ch.25, 8-28 in *Pigs' Meat,* 3 (1795), p.231. "Thus you see", he explained, "God Almighty himself is a very notorious leveller"; *ibid.*
3. *New Sermons to Asses* (London, 1773), p.22, reprinted in *Sermons to Asses.* For a good account of Murray's political views see Knox, "Trumpet of Jubilee", pp.79-80, 82-86.
4. "An Interesting Conversation...", *Pigs' Meat,* 3 (1795), p.234.
5. See, for example, *Restorer,* pp.59-61.
6. See, for example, *ibid.,* pp.63-64.
7. *The Important Trial of Thomas Spence* (London, 1803) reprinted in Waters, *Spence,* p.36. Future references to the *Trial* will be from this Source.
8. *Restorer,* p.54.
9. *The Rights of Infants* (London, 1797) reprinted in Kemp-Ashraf and Mitchell, *William Gallacher,* p.336. Future references to the *Rights of Infants* will be from this source.
10. *Restorer,* pp.42-43.
11. Reprinted in Waters, *Spence,* p.95. Future references to the *Constitution* will be from this source.
12. *A Supplement to the History of Robinson Crusoe* (Newcastle, 1782) reprinted in Kemp-Ashraf and Mitchell, *William Gallacher,* p.306. Future references to the *Supplement* will be from this source.
13. *Constitution,* p.97.
14. "The Marine Republic", *Giant-Killer,* No.2, p.12.
15. *Lecture,* p.15.
16. *Constitution,* p.97.
17. *Ibid.,* p.98. However, women were ineligible for any public employments "in consideration of the delicacy of their sex"; *ibid.*
18. "A Further Account of Spensonia", *Pigs' Meat,* 2 (1794), p.214.
19. *Constitution,* p.95.
20. "A Lesson for the Sheepish Multitude", *Pigs' Meat,* 2 (1794), p.34 (my emphasis).
21. *The Reign of Felicity* (London, 1796), p.10. According to Charles Hall Spence left too many items private property in his revolutionised system: "You leave all this personal property untouched, and consequently, if my suspicions are just, the landed property is only partially divided", "Hall to Spence, August 25th 1807", Add. MSS 27808, f.280. On Hall's developed views see *The Effects of Civilisation* (London, 1805). See also J.R. Dinwiddy, "Charles Hall, Early English Socialist", *International Review of Social History,* 21 (1976), pp.256-276,

22. *Lecture*, pp.5-6.
23. "Spence to Hall, June 28th 1807", Add. MSS 27808, f.284.
24. *Constitution*, p.97.
25. *The Meridian Sun of Liberty* (London, 1796), p.11.
26. "A Dream", *Spence's Songs* (3 parts, London, n.d.), III, n.p.
27. "The Marine Republic", *Giant-Killer*, No.2, p.14.
28. *Restorer*, p.42.
29. *Ibid.*, p.41.
30. *Supplement*, p.305.
31. *Restorer*, p.53.
32. *Supplement*, p.298.
33. "Spence to Hall, June 28th 1807". Hall's reply: "I think we should aim to go back a good way towards our natural state, to that point from which we strayed, retaining but little of that only (to wit of the coarser arts) which civilisation has produced, together with certain sciences"; "Hall to Spence, August 25th 1807".
34. *Restorer*, p.59.
35. "A Dream", n.p.
36. *Restorer*, p.52.
37. "A Dream", n.p. Many of the late eighteenth-century radicals saw luxury, excessive inequality, city life and modern manufacturing with its division of labour as linked with political corruption and social decay. Thus political reform or revolution was seen as a means of "return". There was disagreement, however, on how far one needed to go. Spence saw no contradiction between free trade and artisanal manufacture and a corruptless republic provided that democracy and an agrarian law was secured.

The Structure and Functioning of "Spensonia"

James Harrington[1] was a major influence on Spence. From him he absorbed the notion that there was an intimate connection between economic and political power, thus his insistence on the necessary connection between an agrarian law and democracy. Harrington also provided Spence with an outline of the types of political institutions and practices which would be necessary to avoid corruption and make for a real division of powers. With his own fiercely egalitarian assumptions he re-wrote Harrington's "Oceana" and called it "Spensonia: A Country in Fairyland situated between Utopia and Oceana".[2]

At the centre of "Spensonia" was the Parish. Given the general intellectual, theological and political climate[3] within which Spence had grown up, characterised by extreme hostility towards undemocratic and self-perpetuating centres of state power, it is no surprise that he turned towards the locality. Government, he maintained, should be as close to the people as possible. Such self-government he had experienced in the congregations of which he had been a part and observed in the functioning of local government, guilds, benefit societies and clubs in Newcastle. "It is", he wrote, "to prevent too powerful associations of Citizens so intimately connected that I propose the Land rather to be parochial property than provincial".[4] To allow for genuine self-government each Parish should be "designedly not too large that it may the more easily be managed by the inhabitants with respect to its revenues and police".[5]

After a year's residence every adult man and woman would be a full citizen of the Parish, voting on all matters within it to be conducted by secret ballot. All the land in the Parish would be under collective ownership thus making it the "sovereign lord of its own territories".[6] The land would be rented out, the rent being used "for doing whatever the people think proper; and not as formerly to support and spread luxury, pride and all manner of vice".[7] He made a variety of suggestions (many of which were written into the *Constitution*) about how the revenue raised should be spent. By listing them we can build a picture of how he conceived Parish self-government.

i. Maintaining Parish Officers such as Justices of the Peace and the police.
ii. Building, repairing and adorning houses, bridges and other structures in the Parish.
iii. Making and maintaining passages, highways and canals.
iv. Planting and taking in waste lands.
v. Providing and keeping up ammunition and all sorts of arms.
vi. Granting premiums for agricultural and other improvements.
vii. Providing educational and cultural facilities such as a library, school and assembly rooms.
viii. Maintaining a church and a minister for the religion of the majority, there being freedom of religion for the rest.[8]
ix. Providing a hospital and financing a public health campaign.
x. Constructing safe and convenient bathing places.
xi. Constructing a Public Granary and Fuel Store, the contents to be used in times of need.[9]

There would, therefore, be an active public sector in the Spensonian economy whose functions would be determined by, and whose activities would be controlled by the local communities themselves.

The common ownership of the land was seen to be vital: "If the people wish to have the government in their hands they must begin first by taking the land into their own hands".[10] Private property in the land was not only "the fountainhead of tyranny"[11] but also "the monstrous Hydra of Corruption".[12] He specifically attacked Paine, Thelwall and the philosophers of the French Republic for not seeing this.[13] The right to a share of the land and the right to vote Spence saw as intimately connected:

> "Nobody ought to have a right of suffrage or representation in a society wherein they have no property. As none are suffered to meddle in the affairs of a benefit society or corporation, but those who are members, by having a property therein, none have a right to vote or interfere in the affairs of the government of a country who have no right to the soil, because such are and ought to be accounted strangers."[14]

However, he acknowledged that these reformers saw political change as a *means* to the taxation of estates according to their value, the end of primogeniture, the end of monopolisation in agriculture, and the abolition of the game laws, the aim being to "fashion, reduce, melt and pure down private property".[15]

Spence gave three reasons for rejecting the case for the reform (as opposed to the revolutionisation) of property relations. Firstly, even if there was a jubilee and the land was divided up equally to be passed on to all the children equally, the differential rates of family change and the normal workings of the market would ensure that inequalities re-emerged.[16] Reformers were battling against the tide unless they tackled the root cause of inequality – landlordism. Nor did they account for the fact that the attitudes associated with private property would linger on:

> ". . . pride accompanies Land to such a degree that the Smallest Freeholder is possessed with all the aristocratic haughtiness and contempt for his fellow creatures as the greatest Duke, and is much more insufferable on account of his greater ignorance."[17]

Finally there was a practical, political objection to reformism. For Spence the landed interest was a force which had to be expelled from the body politic before any real change could come about. Leave them intact and they could use their energy, time and money to plot against reform in Parliament.

"When you allow the justice of private property in land", asserted Spence, "you justify everything the landed interest do, both on their own estates and in the Government, for the country is theirs; and what you call oppression, is only their acting consistently with their interest".[18]

Within "Spensonia" agriculture would be the basic economic activity. Each Parish would be like a Board of Agriculture having as its number one priority the provision of agricultural land for all its citizens. As leases expired larger estates would be broken up and waste lands would be enclosed and let for cultivation, country Parishes being under an obligation to invite town dwellers to come and settle on these lands. Loans would be offered if needed.[19] As a result, Spence concluded, "we may suppose that Farms would be so small, and the Farmers would hardly be rich enough to hoard much, neither would they be so few in number as easily to combine to raise the price of their produce".[20] Given the absence of all monopolies "a fair, salutary, and democratic competition will pervade everything".[21]

Each Parish would be obliged to guarantee the right to work. Should anyone find it impossible to employ themselves in a trade or calling or find work as journeymen or labourers then they could apply to the Parish which would either set them to work on the roads or public works or furnish them with land. Should this not be possible within their Parish of residence then "the law provides that they shall be sent to some other parish, where there is room, and be provided as aforesaid".[22] This movement of labour would be an essential feature of Spensonia, helping to ensure that no one Parish monopolises its own advantages: "Our Legislatures will not encourage any narrow, selfish measures".[23]

Two issues of detail clearly bothered Spence: how would the land be distributed? What would be the terms of the lease? On both he underwent a change of mind. In 1782 he envisaged a ballot determining who would gain access to any land for which there was excess demand. The land user, provided he cared for his land, could pass it on to any of his children who had no land. In the case of there being no heirs the land would return to the community.[24] However, in his

London writings he proposed that such land be "let by public auction, after due Advertisement in the Public Prints".[25] This would ensure that the rent found its proper value[26] and, at the same time, any partiality or corruption would be prevented from occurring.[27] At the same time he saw dangers in family tenancies. Thus in an updated version of his lecture he proposed seven-year leases[28] and in his *Constitution* twenty-one year leases.[29] Thus there would be competition for the most desirable leases, the community as a whole gaining through the increased rents that would inevitably result.

Spence recognised that because of the free access to the land, the trading and manufacturing sectors of the economy would be thinned, thus leaving more work for those left behind. The implication was quite simple — higher wages for the remaining workmen.[30] Such workmen would receive their share of the surplus rent and would be provided with housing at reasonable rents.[31] However, on the precise nature of the non-agricultural sector Spence had very little to say. He was aware of the existence of large, joint-stock companies. He specifically mentioned the shipping, colliery, mining and other great concerns of his day whose capital requirements were so great as to require partnership.[32] When we look at his definition of land, which included mines, woods and waters, it is clear that those companies mentioned above would come under parochial ownership. The question remains: how would they be organised in "Spensonia"? In the case of agriculture the land was owned and only ultimately controlled by the community; it was leased out to individual producers. This, it would seem would also be the arrangement for fishing: "I suppose Gentlemen the maritime Parishes would as naturally become Boards of Fisheries as the inland Parishes of Agriculture".[33] The mines, however, would come under direct Parish control, decisions about their use being made in the same way as decisions about waste lands, public transport etc.[34] This would imply that some Parishes were directly involved in commercial activity as public enterprises. The only place where he alludes to this is in the *Supplement* where he notes that Parish revenue will come not only from the rent on the land but also from the sale of timber.[35] Thus the woods would be under direct Parish ownership and control as well.

On trade and manufacturing activities he had even less to say, but when he did it becomes clear that it was small-scale artisanal production and distribution which he had in mind. Wage labour would be an (ultimately) avoidable second-best:

> "In so Prosperous a State as this there would be few labourers or Journeymen in any line of Business. All would be little farmers and little Mastermen. Wages as in America would of consequence be high and where prodigality or mischance did not prevent those hiring themselves might soon be above such necessity."[36]

The whole notion of an economy in which there are many large-scale enterprises with a complex division of labour was alien to Spence's mode of thought. Those that were necessary would be under the direct control of the people.

This still leaves the problem of the point at which rent would be payable by those artisans and tradesmen. Obviously there would be rent on the land and the buildings they used. Spence makes it a community responsibility that workshops be built when an overpopulated Spencean community is spreading to a new area.[37] However, on any machinery that such workshops may contain he is silent. Thus the precise point at which land becomes moveable property is never made clear.[38]

On technical progress Spence is not silent. James Murray had specifically spoken of labour-saving inventions in his sermons. Any man who introduced a machine which replaced labour, he argued, should provide for the men so unemployed.[39] Spence attacked the institution of private patents and proposed instead that Parliament should purchase any "invention or secret" and publish it for common use so long as it was convinced that it would produce no harm: "Thus no quacks or imposters, under pretence of secrets, are suffered to impose on mankind, to ruin their healths or pick their pockets".[40] Thus enterprising men in the arts, sciences and medicine would be rewarded and the community would be in a position to control technical progress.

The Spensonian economy would be a healthy one, avoiding the twin evils of inflation and underconsumption. Prices would be reduced by (1) the removal of paper money — a favourite radical demand, (2) the abolition of all indirect taxes, the payment of rent being the only "charge" laid by the government on the people,[41] and (3) the increased competition that would come with the more equal distribution of the means of production, distribution and exchange. As well as these directly economic causes there would also be community pressure on the producers:

> "The Farmers . . . would not be the last to show a disposition to supply the Markets at a reasonable Rate. For they must thenceforth look on the People as their Landlords, who either might renew their Leases or not, as they considered them well-wishers to the Public Good."[42]

In fact prices would be pushed down so much that Spensonian producers would out-compete all their rivals on the world market. Thus other nations would be forced to adopt a Spencean system if they were to remain as viable economies. In this way Spencean principles would spread to all corners of the world.[43]

For the domestic economy to be fully healthy, however, it was also necessary for the wealth producers (the labouring classes) to be the consumers. In contemporary, class-divided society the rich, that is the landlord class, were "most tardy" as consumers and "many of them such retentive Leeches, that they seem to require some of the aforesaid Stimulants,[44] or Emetics, to make them disgorge, and give back to the Life's Blood of Society, which their Tenacity retains from Circulation".[45] He compared "Spensonia" to a "benign and sudden spring to the frost-bitten Earth, after a long and severe Winter". It would guarantee "a continual flow of permanent Wealth".[46]

A portion of the rent would also go towards the financing of County and National Government. It would be sent quarterly, being based on a pound rate of the rents raised in each Parish.[47] However, the powers of such governments were to be limited by a system of checks and balances. Nevertheless they were an essential part of "Spensonia, being needed, firstly, to resolve any inter-Parish disputes, secondly, to deal with matters that could not be dealt with at a Parish level, and, thirdly, to make sure that no one Parish broke the laws of nature of which they were supposed to be the embodiment.

At the national level the Legislature, Executive and Administration would be radically separate.[48] The Legislature (or National Assembly) would be elected annually by the individuals in each Parish or, if there were more than one thousand Parishes, by especially constituted electoral districts. It would pass decrees and propose laws, both civil and criminal. Such laws would only come into effect if in more than one-half of all the Counties, one-tenth of all the Parishes had not objected. The National Assembly would also determine the number and functions of the nation's General Administration and the functions and rules of organisation for the County Administrations. It also appointed (from outside its own ranks) the Commissioner of the National Treasury and the Executive Council. The latter would be chosen from a general list presented to it by the County Electoral Assemblies. One half of the Executive Council would retire each year, just before the end of the Assembly's annual session.

The Executive Council would choose (from outside its own ranks) the General Administration and the nation's external agents. It would also appoint the National Treasury and negotiate treaties (to be ratified by the National Assembly). "It cannot", Spence stressed, "act but in Execution of Laws, and Decrees of the Legislative Body".[49] The Executive would, however, have the right to be admitted to the National Assembly to be "heard as often as it has an account to give".[50]

The individual Parishes would also elect annually two delegates to a County Electoral Assembly, each of which would nominate two members for the general list of Spensonians from which the Executive is chosen by the National Assembly. Every six months the County Assemblies would choose County Administrators (whose functions would be determined by the National Assembly) and every twelve months Public Arbitrators and Criminal Judges to deal with matters too complex for the local Justices of the Peace (elected in each Parish). A national Tribunal of Appeal would also exist, to be chosen by the Electoral Assemblies together.

Spence also made provision for constitutional reform. If in more than one half of the Counties, one tenth of the Parishes indicated that they wanted some change then an Assembly of Constitutional Revision would be formed on the basis of two members from each County Electoral Assembly. They would draft a proposal for reform and send it back to the Parishes for approval or rejection.

Thus, in "Spensonia", the powers of the National Government would be severely restricted, ultimately by the Parish control over its revenue and expenditure. Spence explained:

> ". . . a Government that draws great Riches from sources which do not immediately affect the people, as from Loans, Mines, Foreign Tribute or Subsidies is sure to creep by Degrees into absolute power and overturn everything.
> It is for this reason I would not have the Land national, nor provincial, but parochial property, that the People might be as much interested as possible, both in the improvement of their estates, which would thus be always under their eye, and in the expenditure of all public monies, which would be paid straight out of their Revenues, even while in their hands, and when just going into their pockets."[51]

Two other features of government throughout "Spensonia" would also guarantee liberty and prevent the re-emergence of tyranny: voting by secret ballot and the universal use of arms. These were its "guardian angels".[52] The former would prevent corruption and give everyone a stake in the system. The latter would allow the people to assert their right of insurrection should the Government violate the rights of man. "Thus each Parish", wrote Spence, "is a little polished Athens, as well as a warlike Sparta".[53]

Spence also introduced the idea that with the establishment of his principles the whole nature of politics would be transformed from the administration of *people* to the administration of *things*:

> "Instead of debating about mending the state, as with you, (for ours needs no mending) we employ our ingenuity nearer home, and the result of our debates are in every parish, how we shall work such a

mine, make such a river navigable, drain such a fen, or improve such a waste. These things we are all immediately interested in, and each have a vote in executing."[54]

He saw his system as nothing less than a synthesis of the Millenium of religion, the Age of Reason of Philosophy and the Golden Age of poetry.[55] It would be perfectly balanced and therefore permanent. Society would be united under one interest, industry would be relieved of all fetters and peace would allow men and women to enjoy the blessings of nature unhindered. Nothing less but nothing more, a system of law being required to deal with those possessing vicious inclinations.[56]

In describing the new society and in calling the people to revolt against the old one Spence was dependent on biblical imagery and prophecy — that was the language and symbolism within which he presented his ideas.[57] Nevertheless he distanced himself from Christianity in particular and religion in general. The idea of justice in the Old Testament, he informed the court in 1801, did not come up to his own standards.[58] Nor was religion the means to salvation:

> "You see I do not in the old fashioned manner attempt to preach and pray the World into Justice and Tenderheartedness. No truly. I have seen enough of that kind of delusion. If Religion would have any influence on Men's Lives, we ought to be the most righteous and compassionate people on Earth."[59]

How then was the Spencean revolution to occur? It is to this problem that I now turn.

Footnotes

1. For a recent study see James Cotton, "James Harrington as Aristotelian", *Political Theory*, 7 (1979), pp.371-389.
2. The *Constitution* was constructed from the French Constitution of 1793 which was drafted but not implemented. Spence superimposed his own ideas over those of the French. See J.H. Stewart, *A Documentary Survey of the French Revolution* (New York, 1951), pp.454-472. Spence was highly critical of More's *Utopia* for making "every kind of property the property of the nation and the People obliged to work under gang-masters"; "Spence to Hall, June 28th 1807".
3. On the Newcastle background to Spence's thought see Knox, "Trumpet of Jubilee", pp.78-87 and Kemp-Ashraf, "Thomas Spence", pp.278-279, 283-284.
4. *Restorer*, p.37.

5. *Constitution*, p.99.
6. *Lecture*, p.11.
7. *Ibid.*, p.12.
8. Spence only made this proposal in his *Supplement*, p.306. There is no mention of it in the *Constitution*.
9. For details of all these proposals see *Lecture*, pp.11-12; *Supplement*, pp.305-306; *Restorer*, pp.43-54, 61-62; and *Constitution*, pp.99-102.
10. "A Further Account", p.215.
11. *Ibid.*
12. *Trial*, p.74.
13. On the ideas of the English Jacobins in the 1790s see Dickinson, *Liberty and Property*, Ch.7. On the movement see Gwyn A. Williams, *Artisans and Sans-Culottes* (London, 1968).
14. *Meridian Sun*, p.2.
15. *Ibid.*, p.3.
16. "A Further Account", p.216.
17. *Restorer*, p.49.
18. *Meridian Sun*, p.4. See also *The End of Oppression* (2nd ed.; London, 1796) reprinted in Kemp-Ashraf and Mitchell, *William Gallacher*, pp.312-313. Future references to *End of Oppression* will be from this source.
19. *Restorer*, p.59.
20. *Ibid.*, p.44.
21. *Rights of Infants*, appendix, p.14 (the appendix is not reprinted in Kemp-Ashraf and Mitchell).
22. "The Marine Republic", *Giant-Killer*, No.2, p.12.
23. *Ibid.*, p.14.
24. *Supplement*, p.305.
25. *Constitution*, p.100.
26. *Ibid.*, p.99.
27. "The Marine Republic", *Giant-Killer*, No.1, p.2.
28. *Meridian Sun*, p.11.
29. *Constitution*, p.99. Two points should be added. Spence proposed the banning of sub-leasing except where an innkeeper or private person gave accommodation to others; *ibid.*, p.100. Nor was he opposed to one person holding more than one lease: ". . . a person's health or business may require him to occupy Tenements in different situations at the same time; as for instance, in both town and country: or he may wish to secure the possession of some desirable tenement, that is to let before the lease of the place he holds at present expires"; *ibid.*, pp.100-101. A person could, however, only be a citizen of one Parish.
30. *Restorer*, p.59.
31. *Constitution*, p.100. The Parish would also provide such housing for "widows and others who desire and require but little room"; *ibid.*
32. "A Dream", n.p.
33. *Restorer*, p.59.
34. "A Further Account", p.214.
35. *Supplement*, p.304.
36. "Spence to Hall, June 28th 1807". On the background see C. Hill, "Pottage for Freeborn Englishmen: Attitudes to Wage Labour in the Sixteenth and Seventeenth Centuries", in C.H. Feinstein (ed.) *Socialism, Capitalism and Economic Growth Essays Presented to Maurice Dobb* (Cambridge, 1967), pp.338-350.

37. "The Marine Republic", *Pigs' Meat*, 2 (1794), p.81.
38. Kemp-Ashraf has claimed that for Spence pre-Industrial Revolution technology would remain private property but all large enterprises using modern methods of production and with a complex division of labour would be public property and if not managed by the Parish directly they would be run as worker co-operatives. For evidence of Spence's belief in co-operatives she points to his "Marine Republic" where he describes life on board a ship and later on an island organised along Spencean lines. She argues that this is not only meant to be an allegory for the Parish Republics but a model for organising any enterprise with a complex division of labour; "Thomas Spence", pp.272-273. However, the only time he refers to large-scale activities — mining — he has it under Parish control. In "A Dream" he did show that he was aware of large joint-stock companies but as in "Marine Republic" he referred to them as allegories for parish self-management. On modern machine technology Spence was silent; his economy was to be one of small farmers, artisans and traders. Kemp-Ashraf is too keen to make the concerns of nineteenth-century socialism Spence's concerns.
39. *New Sermons*, p.22.
40. "A Further Account", p.218.
41. *Restorer*, p.58. It should also be noted that Spence advocated the repudiation of the National Debt. The "Stockholders", he argued, would lose their "Money in the Funds" as a result of the revolution; *ibid.*, p.55.
42. *Ibid.*, p.58.
43. *Ibid.*, p.59. Spence also has a place for direct conquest. When over-population set in in the home country expansion overseas was justified. However, as soon as the colonies had adopted a Spencean constitution they were to be granted their independence. See "Marine Republic", *Giant-Killer*, No.2, p.13 and *Constitution*, pp.108-109.
44. By these he meant fires, shipwrecks, wars and all external stimulants to economic activity.
45. "A New and Infallible Way to Make Trade", *Spence's Songs*, III, n.p. The source here is clearly Murray, *New Sermons*, pp.19-20.
46. *End of Oppression*, p.314.
47. In the *Lecture* he proposed that each Parish pay an equal amount; p.13. In the *Constitution*, obviously to make payment proportional to riches, he proposed that each Parish contribute a percentage of what they collect; p.107.
48. See M.J.C. Vile, *Constitutionalism and the Separation of Powers* (Oxford, 1967) Chs.1-4 for the background. Spence adhered to the strong version of the doctrine believing that the functions of government (legislative, executive and judicial) should be so separate that no one person can exercise more than one function.
49. *Constitution*, p.104.
50. *Ibid.*, p.105.
51. *Restorer*, p.52.
52. "A Further Account", p.215.
53. *Supplement*, p.305. In the *Lecture* Spence opposed the existence of a standing army; p.14. However, in the *Constitution* he makes provision for both a standing army and navy. They were to be under democratic control and all Spensonians would be armed and trained to resist them if they tried to impose military rule; p.107.

54. "A Further Account", p.214. Spence was writing as a Spensonian citizen.
55. *Trial*, p.35.
56. *The Case of Thomas Spence* (London, 1792), p.11.
57. See Parssinen, "Land Nationalisation", p.140 and Knox, "Trumpet of Jubilee", pp.79-81.
58. *Trial*, p.65.
59. *Restorer*, p.58.

The Transition

In the *Lecture* Spence had simply spoken of the "whole people", after much deliberation and reasoning, coming to the conclusion that a new society founded on Spencean principles was necessary and on a day appointed (by whom he does not say) deciding to bring it into being.[1] Nothing is said on the possibility of landlord reaction or on the questions of co-ordination and organisation during the transition. This, argues Knox, remained the case, Spence's "biblical imagery" being "the substance of social chance":

> "The change did not depend on Divine intervention; it was to be carried out by those in the social depths. Yet it is almost completely devoid of conflict in the event or after. And it is almost completely free as well of concern with organisation that would follow from an expectation of conflict."[2]

Certainly the biblical imagery is there — promulgation of the "Plan" giving way to the preparation of society at large which would be followed by the decisive break with the past. However, Knox's claim that Spence's account is "almost completely" lacking in concern for conflict and organisation is based on a too selective reading of the sources.[3] Such concerns were part and parcel of all of Spence's writings on the transition.

Three assumptions underpinned all but one of his commentaries on the question. Firstly, he linked analyses of chance with a notion of "crisis":

> "When I contemplate the meagre and beggarly appearance of the working people at this deplorable period, and at the same time hear

their deep and desperate exclamations, sighed forth from their broken hearts, I cannot help thinking but that we are on the eve of some very great commotion."[4]

The landlord class and their allies, desirous of establishing an international as well as a national monopoly of trade, had intensified their exploitation and oppression of the people.[5] In such a situation some sort of rebellion was inevitable, the only question that remained concerned the *direction* it would take. Spence envisaged a process of permanent revolutionary upheaval until society had been re-structured on the right principles: "Revolutions will now never cease, or rather the Nations will be in a continual state of Revolution, till perfect Truth and Right be established".[6]

Secondly, he believed that the possibility of landlord reaction had to be taken into account. "Every government founded on injustice", he wrote, "is and must be, a military government in some degree". Thus "Spensonianism could not be established where other governments had been before without an Army".[7] In a poem, "The Downfall of Feudal Tyranny", written while in Newgate Prison in 1794, he spoke of the landlord reaction to the spread of Spencean ideas:

> Observe how they fly now to arms,
> For Mankind they see, are resolved to be free,
> Which ev'ry tyrant alarms...[8]

However, "sad ruin's their fate, though they associate".[9]

Thirdly, he spoke of the transition in the context of massive support for his ideas:

> "... who would suppose that only a few Parishes would be so foolhardy, as to set up a New System, so contrary to former Prejudices and Interests without well knowing that the whole Nation were ripe and ready to join them?"[10]

Most of Spence's time was spent trying to bring about this mass support for his ideas. He often despaired at the propensity of human beings to allow themselves to be oppressed. The frustration he felt was often acute. He even dismissed Burke's description of the masses as "the swinish multitude". "On very slight observation", he noted, "he would find real Swine to be more noble animals, and far from being so obsequeous". Hogs did not quietly suffer want, nor would they be herded into armies to fight and kill one another.[11] The problem of winning the people over to the cause was aggravated by the activities of the wealthy who not only tried to prevent "the union of the people" but also "the light from spreading". To do this they had much time, energy and money.[12]

Nevertheless, despite these obstacles, Spence believed that the time would come when the people would see that the solution to their problems lay with his plan: sufficient reason existed within the human condition for them to see its relevance,[13] the conditions under which the people lived was getting worse and forcing them to move from considering "which form of Government is most favourable to Liberty" to the question of "which System of Society is most favourable to existence",[14] and modern methods of communication were making it easier to spread ideas:

> ". . . by means of Printing all Nations as well as individuals and Parishes, learn everything of a General Tendency at the same time . . ."[15]

And in any case nothing but a revolution from below could be guaranteed to produce the results. He attacked those radicals who addressed themselves to "the religion, generosity, and feelings of the rich and powerful, for their humiliating charity". Despite all the preaching about "justice and tender-heartedness" oppression and monopoly had nowhere been overcome by these means.[16]

Spence's belief in the revolutionary potential of the people was not nurtured in isolation from a tradition of autonomous working-class action in the North East. Spence even used the term "Mutiny on the Land"[17] which was "commonly used for the strikes of the miners and keelmen in the North and for other popular disturbances".[18] That he drew lessons from these experiences is also clear. Because the people had to labour to live they could never maintain themselves for very long in "a state of Insurrection against their Oppressors":

> "They must away to their work again. The cries of their famished Families break up their Campaigns before they are well begun, and

they must again return to the yoke, like starved animals, for mere subsistence."[19]

The conclusion to be drawn by Spencean revolutionaries was clear: the working people should, as soon as possible in their revolution, take control of the resources of war and the land (including the last payments of rent to the old landlords) so that they can successfully wage their struggle.[20]

Given, then, a crisis in which the mass of the people had come to see the truth of Spencean principles, how would the final transition occur? In the *End of Oppression* he spoke of "a few Thousands of hearty determined Fellows well armed and appointed with Officers, and having a Committee of honest, firm, and intelligent Men to act as a provisionary Government, and to direct their Actions to the proper Object".[21] They would publish a manifesto and direct the people in the Parishes to take possession of the landed property therein, appointing a committee to manage the process of change. If the "Aristocracy arose to contend the matter, let the People be firm and desperate, destroying them Root and Branch, and strengthening their Hands by the rich Confiscations".[22]

In the *Restorer* the process is described differently. A few contingent Parishes, wrote Spence, would declare the land to be theirs and form "a convention of Parochial Delegates". Other Parishes would be invited to follow the example and send delegates to what was in effect a National Assembly.[23] Should the landed interest stir the people would be compelled to "exterminate them and sequester also the Remainder of their illgotten Wealth".[24] In other words they would lose their land, their lives *and* their moveable property. In the case of non-resistance the moveable property would stay with the landlords, enabling them "to maintain themselves luxuriously, without Work or Industry all their Lives, especially in a Nation where everything will be cheap, and free of Taxes".[25]

In the *Giant-Killer* version of "The Marine Republic" Spence mentioned the revolutionary army again, arguing that it would only need to be small as there would be massive support for Spencean ideas. The army would simply be "aiding the establishment of Justice".[26]

In his first account of the transition the army and provisional government had a starting, organising and co-ordinating role to play. Most of the action, however, would occur at the Parish level, it being the self-activity of the people already imbued with Spencean principles. In 1801 the revolution is given an even more spontaneous character. Indeed Spence referred to the American and French Revolutions and the recent mutinies of the fleets[27] in England as evidence of the "public spirit, and extensive unanimity in the present generation to accomplish Schemes of infinitely greater difficulty than a thing that may be done in a Day, when once the public mind is duly prepared".[28] Thus the starting, organising and co-ordinating functions would be performed in the Parishes themselves and in co-operation through the Convention of Parochial Delegates (embryo National Assembly). When he did mention the army again in 1814 it was simply an aid to the revolutionary process.

It is clear, then, that Spence did take account of the possibility of conflict. As far as was possible he wanted to avoid violence: "Here is no Tocsin sounded as a signal for massacre no war-whoop for an ignorant Rabble to turn out and burn and destroy".[29] He saw it as an attempt to attain rights by unanimity and order. Only if the people knew and truly understood the principles on which they were acting was this possible. It was Spence's belief that the people could be so educated and transformed into a self-organised and disciplined force for change.

However, in one of his tracts he presented the transition in a completely different light. In *A Fragment of Ancient Prophecy* (1796) he developed the following scenario for Europe. Quite clearly it was meant to be an allegory for contemporary events. Firstly he spoke of the revolution which established a democratic and republican form of government and the counter-revolution of the old ruling class of Europe prompted by the fear that the "genuine" principles of liberty (that is Spenceanism) will spread with the "fictitious". However, the "Country of Liberty" will beat off this challenge and start to spread the new system of government. Undeterred the old ruling class will continue to fight, making the expenses of war for the country of liberty ever greater. At this point a solution would be offered to them by a citizen of "the Island" which has fallen to the revolutionary forces:

> "... the Man of the Island, who publishes the real System of Liberty, will speak unto them, saying, Take possession of all the rents of the conquered countries, and they will be more than sufficient to pay your armies, and do ye also abolish all the taxes which their governments had imposed on the people."[30]

At the end of the war this "preacher" would then call on the conquering nation to give back to the conquered their national independence. Eventually the country of liberty would establish the system as well.

It would seem that at this time Spence was particularly frustrated by his lack of success. He came to pin his hopes on a French invasion and what he saw as the inevitable logic that would follow. An indication of his frustration and pessimism can be seen from his proposal, outlined at roughly the same time, that women be the administrators in "Spensonia". Like "he-asses" the men "suffer themselves to be laden with as many pair of panyers of rents, tythes, etc., as your *tender* consciences please to lay upon them".[31]

Thus:

> "... we women (because the men are not to be depended on) will appoint, in every parish, a committee of our own sex (which we presume our gallant lock-jawed spouses and paramours will at least, for their own interest, not oppose) to receive the rents ..."[32]

He then went on to describe the general administration of the Parish. In other words one-half of the population would rule the other half.

As a result of his frustration in the late 1790s Spence came to question both the notions of a popular revolution and a popular democracy. He may well have contemplated a Babeuf-type dictatorship as a means of bringing about a revolution in a society "under the influence" of the ruling class,[33] but neither his theory or practice indicates that he did in any serious way. Nor did he become involved with those who were actively planning for a French invasion.[34]

However, by the turn of the century any ambiguities in Spence's account of the transition had vanished. His post-1800 writings expressed a re-vitalised confidence in the common people to be a force for change. At the same time any hopes he may have had about the French being an agent of Spenceanism were quickly dispelled. The French Revolution, he told Hall, had been a "Miscarriage".[35] Because it had left "Giantism still in Substance" a new class of "Giants" arose to begin its retrograde motion.[36] The fact that Spence had attracted some followers to his Plan must also have cheered him.

In part, then, Knox is right to describe Spence as nothing more than a "radical crank".[37] He did have a rather utopian notion of the way his ideas would spread and he was too obsessed with his own Plan and the inflexible relationship between political and social change which it assumed. Nevertheless Spence was not simply another millenarian or utopian. He did have some notion of what a revolution would require and he was critical of those who would try to act before the "time was ripe". Thus there is an element of modern revolutionism in his thought. With a certain degree of consciousness, but not a great deal of success, Spence was trying to take both the working people beyond their traditional and limited concerns[38] and the millenarian and utopian traditions out of their ghetto and into the age of democratic politics which was taking shape. In an important sense this has always been the major challenge facing modern socialists.

Footnotes

1. *Lecture*, p.10.
2. "Trumpet of Jubilee", pp.94, 96-97. Francis Place tells a similar story in his unpublished memoir. Except to criticise Spence for his failure to take account of population growth Place makes no reference to his ideas. He concerned himself with the man ("sincere and childlike . . . impractical in the ways of the world") and his society ("there was no such society and scarcely a hope, or any expectation of the ability to form a society"); Add. MSS, ff.152, 204. The evidence certainly indicates that the latter claim is wrong (see Rudkin, *Thomas Spence,* Ch.6) whilst the former is simply Place's assessment of Spence the man and, by implication, his style of politics, towards which he had little sympathy. On Place as a source see Thompson, *Working Class,* pp.147, 530-531, 672-673. It should also be

remembered that Place was no dealer in ideas. See W.E.S. Thomas, "Francis Place and the Working Class", *Historical Journal*, 5 (1962), p.63.
3. For a fuller treatment see Kemp-Ashraf, "Thomas Spence", pp.280-284. She places Spence in the context of a tradition of working class self-organisation and action in the North-East. This is the one aspect of the Newcastle background to Spence's thought which Knox's otherwise excellent account leaves out.
4. *Restorer*, p.63.
5. *Ibid.*, pp.46, 51.
6. *Ibid.*, p.64.
7. "The Marine Republic", *Giant-Killer*, No.2, p.13.
8. *Pigs' Meat*, 3 (1795), p.251.
9. *Ibid.*
10. *Restorer*, p.48.
11. "The Rights of Man, by Question and Answer, *Pigs' Meat*, 1 (1793), p.263.
12. *End of Oppression*, p.312.
13. "Rights of Man", p.265.
14. *Restorer*, p.64.
15. *Ibid.*, p.48.
16. *Ibid.*, p.58.
17. *Ibid.*, p.48.
18. Kemp-Ashraf, "Thomas Spence", p.283.
19. *End of Oppression*, p.313.
20. *Ibid.*, pp.313-314.
21. *Ibid.* This tract was written in the form of a dialogue between an old and a young Spencean mechanic. The young man asked the old: "Let us suppose that a whole Nation . . . were fully convinced of the excellence of this System, and universally wishing its establishment, I should be glad to know the most easy method of doing so, with least bloodshed".
22. *Ibid.*, p.314.
23. *Restorer*, pp.47-48.
24. *Ibid.*, p.55. Thus the physical extermination of the landlords was conditional upon their resisting the revolution. Parssinen, incorrectly I think, makes it a necessary part of the transition; "Land Nationalisation", p.139.
25. *Restorer*, p.55.
26. "The Marine Republic", *Giant-Killer*, No.2, p.13.
27. At Spithead and Nore in 1797. Thus the Report of the House of Commons Committee in 1801 which accused the "Spensonian Society" of desiring to achieve Spence's Plan "by a general insurrection of the people, for which the revolutionary outrages in France and the Mutiny in our own Fleet are held out as laudable examples" was not too wide of the mark; Add. MSS 27808, f.202. It does indicate Spence's view. However, on whether a Spensonian Society existed in 1801 the evidence is not so clear.
28. *Restorer*, p.48.
29. *Ibid.*
30. *Fragment*, p.4.
31. *Rights of Infants*, p.331.
32. *Ibid.*, pp.333-334.
33. Babeuf wanted a temporary dictatorship because he believed the majority to be under the influence of the Directory and Royalists and therefore enemies of liberty. See R.B. Rose, "Gracchus Babeuf", *Encounter*, July 1976, pp.28-36.

34. On the question of French invasion and the radicals see Marianne Elliot, "The 'Despard Conspiracy' Reconsidered", *Past and Present,* No.75 (1977), pp.46-61 and Goodwin, *Friends of Liberty,* Ch.11.
35. "Spence to Hall, June 28th 1807".
36. *Giant-Killer,* No.1, pp.6-7.
37. "Trumpet of Jubilee", p.75.
38. By this I mean the so-called "moral economy of the crowd". See Thompson, *Working Class,* Ch.3 and George Rudé, *The Crowd in History: A Study of Popular Disturbance in France and England 1730-1848* (New York, 1964).

Conclusion

Spence's importance lies in certain, and to varying degrees, original aspects of his thought which he developed and his followers kept alive, at least until 1840.[1] He played his part, admittedly small, in "the making of the working class".[2] Firstly we can point to his belief in the potential of the common people, not just as the source for a new, highly participatory democracy but also as a revolutionary force.[3] Spence saw in popular uprisings not anarchy and disorder but the embryo of a highly disciplined and organised force for change. His conception of the act of revolution via a "Union of the People" at parish and national levels was a further development of the radical idea that the people had a right to elect a national convention which was not just a device to put pressure on parliament but an alternative source of authority.[4] He differed from them, however, in that he wanted to fuse the political and the social demands in the process of revolution itself. Both the state and the land (and its appurtenances) were to be seized by the people and reconstituted under their ownership and control.

Secondly Spence helped, albeit in an indirect way in that his specific analysis of class was anything but systematic, in the formation of a distinctly socialist conception of class.[5] Most of the radicals saw politics as a struggle between an aristocratic clique (exercising their power through a corrupt parliament) and the people, excessive taxation and an oppressive legal system being the chief causes of division in society. For Spence and his followers, on the other hand, the private property system (established by conquest) was the cause of inequality and poverty. They argued that without community ownership and control of the land and its appurtenances political reform, cheap government and an unbiassed legal system would be worthless. For them the ownership system was decisive, all else was derivative: ". . . the Laws are made by Property; and for Property. Men then are out of the question except as appendages to this same Property".[6]

Finally Spence was the first radical of his generation to develop a socialist critique of wage labour and advocate common ownership.[7] For most of the other radicals such ideas were only raised to be refuted. Spence's alternative was to be based on an economy of small farmers and artisan manufacturers leasing their land and workshops from the community. However, it was not just to be a republic of small producers and exchange relations but a federation of small, self-governing communities exercising ultimate control over the economic process and caring for each of its members.[8] Decentralisation, participation and mutuality were to be central features. In other words Spence was *the* socialist theorist of his generation and deserves his place in the history of British political thought for this reason alone. From a critical and analytical point of view the contributions of Hall and Godwin were probably more important; Hall developing the conceptual equipment for a critique of capitalism and Godwin the philosophical and ethical underpinnings for socialist social relations. However, from a constructive and synthetic point of view Spence led the way, being the first to attempt an integration of democratic republicanism, communitarianism and popular revolutionism. With S.F. Markham we may call him Britain's "first modern socialist".[9]

Footnotes

1. For evidence of Spenceanism in the 1830s see P. Hollis, *The Pauper Press: A Study in Working Class Radicalism of the 1830s* (Oxford, 1970), pp.211-214.
2. Rudkin claimed that Spence was the chief influence behind Owen. She noted similarities between the thought of the two and then leapt to the conclusion that Owenism was Spenceanism refined; *Thomas Spence,* Ch.9. The dangers in such an approach when there were so many shared assumptions and a complex interplay of ideas has been well argued by Prothero. "William Benbow".

3. William Godwin and Charles Hall, whose conception of the utopian society came closest to Spence's, both rejected popular action from below. See Hall, *Effects*, Ch.XXX and William Godwin, *Enquiry Concerning Political Justice* (3rd ed., London, 1798), Book IV, Ch.2.
4. See Prothero, "William Benbow" and T.W. Parssinen, "Association, Convention and Anti-Parliament in British Politics", *English Historical Review* 88 (1973), pp.504-533.
5. On notions of class in this period see P.H. Ilis (ed.), *Class and Class Conflict in nineteenth-century England 1815-1850* (London and Boston, 1973), Part I.
6. *Trial*, p.69.
7. For similar conceptions of the new society see Hall, *Effects*, Chs.XXXVII-XXXVIII, Godwin, *Political Justice,* Book VIII, and S.T. Coleridge, *Lectures 1795 On Politics and Religion,* ed. Lewis Patten and Peter Mann (London, 1971). John Thelwall, although he rejected common ownership and had a place for modern factories in his future society, was the most advanced of the mainstream radicals. See his *The Rights of Nature* . . . (London, 1796) and *The Tribune,* 3 vols (London, 1796). It should also be noted that Robert Wallace had presented (and supported) the strictly ethical case for a communist utopia only to conclude that it would hasten overpopulation and misery; *Various Prospects of Mankind, Nature and Providence* (London, 1761).
8. As Patricia Hollis puts it: "Where the men of 1819 saw the model society as a fragmented bundle of individuals the Spencean farming parish was more nearly communitarian"; *Pauper Press,* p.214. By the "men of 1819" she means the mainstream radicals who saw corruption, excessive taxation, oppressive laws and priestcraft as the causes of division and discontent in society.
9. *A History of Socialism* (London, 1930), p.2.

Bibliography

Thomas Spence: A Bibliography of tracts and articles (short titles).
The Real Reading Made Easy (Newcastle, 1782).
A Supplement to the History of Robinson Crusoe (Newcastle, 1782).
The Case of Thomas Spence, Bookseller (London, 1792).
The Rights of Man (London, 1793).
One Pennyworth of Pigs' Meat, Vols.I, II, III (London, 1793, 4, 5).
"The Rights of Man, by Question and Answer", *Pigs' Meat,* I, p.9, 261-7.
"A Lesson for the Sheepish Multitude", *Pigs' Meat,* II, pp.32-5.
"The Marine Republic", *Pigs' Meat,* II, pp.68-72.
"A Further Account of Spensonia", *Pigs' Meat,* II, pp.205-18.
"The Real Rights of Man", *Pigs' Meat,* III, pp.220-29.
"An Interesting Conversation", *Pigs' Meat,* III, pp.229-39.
End of Oppression (London, 1795).
Recantation of the End of Oppression (London, 1795).
A Letter from Ralph Hodge to his cousin Thomas Bull (London, 1795).
Meridian Sun of Liberty (London, 1796).
Reign of Felicity (London, 1796).
A Fragment of Ancient Prophecy (London, 1796).
Rights of Infants (London, 1797).
Constitution of a Perfect Commonwealth (London, 1798).
Restorer of Society to its Natural State (London, 1801).
Constitution of Spensonia (London, 1803).

THOMAS SPENCE

The Important Trial of Thomas Spence (London, 1803).
Spence's Songs, parts I, II, III (London, n.d.).
"A Dream", *Songs,* III.
"A New and Infallible Way to make Trade", *Songs,* III.
The Giant-Killer or Anti-Landlord, Nos.1 and 2 (London, 1814).
"The Marine Republic", *Giant-Killer,* No.1 (pp.1-2) and No.2 (pp.12-14).

II
Selected Writings

Introductory Notes

The Rights of Man (1793) is the fourth edition of Spence's lecture to the Newcastle Philosophical Society, first delivered in 1775. Unfortunately the first three editions cannot be traced. Appended to the lecture, and included in this collection, is "An Interesting Conversation between a Gentleman and the Author". In most of his tracts Spence used a dialogue or conversation, usually between a member of the upper class sceptical of Spencean principles or a labourer eager for enlightenment and a wise old Spencean, to present his arguments.

Spence's periodical publication, *Pigs' Meat* (1793-95), was published and sold weekly for one penny. Each year they were compiled in bound volumes and sold in that form. Contained within *Pigs' Meat* were mostly extracts from other writers, both classical and modern. However, several essays, songs and poems by Spence were also included. "The Marine Republic" and "A Further Account of Spensonia" were both published in Volume II (1794). In these two essays Spence used the traditional utopian method to describe life on an island organised along Spencean lines. Other descriptions of "Spensonia" can be found in *A Supplement to the History of Robinson Crusoe* (1782) and "The Marine Republic", 2 parts, *Giant-Killer* (1814).

In 1795 Spence published two editions of his *End of Oppression* in which he outlined for the first time his views on the revolutionary process itself. Included in this collection is the lengthier second edition.

A Letter from Ralph Hodge (1795) was clearly intended as a parody of *One Pennyworth of Truth from Thomas Bull to his Brother John* issued for popular consumption by John Reeve's Society for Preserving Liberty and Property Against Republicans and Levellers. In it he joins in the radical complaints about the taxation and funding systems. Cheap and honest government, as well as common ownership and equality, were to be features of "Spensonia".

The Meridian Sun of Liberty (1796) is the sixth edition of the 1775 lecture. Included in this collection is the preface in which Spence describes very clearly his objections to the politics of Paine, Thelwall and the mainstream radicals. This is a theme continued in *The Rights of Infants* (1797) where Spence specifically deals with Paine's *Agrarian Justice.* For Spence the issues of politics and property were linked in a way unrecognised by the mainstream radicals.

The Restorer of Society (1801) contains the most thorough and comprehensive exposition of Spence's ideas. It was this tract that led to his trial in the same year. After his release from prison he republished it as he had read it out to the court during his defence. To the original he added various comments as footnotes to clarify his views. It is this edition (of 1803, reprinted again in 1807) which is included in this collection.

The Constitution of Spensonia (1803) is an amended and longer version of the *Constitution of a Perfect Commonwealth* (1798). It is based on the French Constitution of 1793 — published in full in Volume II of *Pigs' Meat.* Included here is the fourth edition of the *Constitution* originally published in phonetics (1803) but reprinted in ordinary spelling in *The Important Trial* (1807 ed.).

Eccentricites of grammar and spelling have been left untouched.

G.I. Gallop

The Rights of Man (1793)

A Lecture
Read at the Philosophical Society in Newcastle on November 8th, 1775, for printing of which the Society did the Author the Honour to expel him

Mr President, It being my turn to lecture, I beg to give some thoughts on this important question, viz. — Whether mankind in society reap all the advantages from their natural and equal rights of property in land and liberty, which in that state they possibly may and ought to expect? And as I hope you, Mr President and the good company here, are sincere friends to truth, I am under no apprehensions of giving offence by defending her cause with freedom.

That property in land and liberty among men in a state of nature ought to be equal, few, one would be fain to hope, would be foolish enough to deny. Therefore, taking this to be granted, the country of any people, in a native state, is properly their common, in which each of them has an equal property, with free liberty to sustain himself and family with the animals, fruits and other products thereof. Thus such a people reap jointly the whole advantages of their country, or neighbourhood, without having their right in so doing called in question by any, not even by the most selfish and corrupt. For upon what must they live if not upon the productions of the country in which they reside? Surely, to deny them that right is in effect denying them a right to live. Well, methinks some are now ready to say, but is it lawful, reasonable and just, for this people to sell, or make a present even, of the whole of their country, or common, to whom they will, to be held by them and their heirs for ever?

To this I answer, if their posterity require no grosser materials to live and move upon than air, it would certainly be very ill-natured to dispute their right of parting, for what of their own, their posterity would never have occasion for; but if their posterity cannot live but as grossly as they do, the same gross materials must be left them to live upon. For the right to deprive anything of the means of living, supposes a right to deprive it of life; and this right ancestors are not supposed to have over their posterity.

Hence it is plain that the land or earth, in any country or neighbourhood, with everything in or on the same, or pertaining thereto, belongs at all times to the living inhabitants of the said country or neighbourhood in an equal manner. For, as I said before, there is no living but on land and its productions, consequently, what we cannot live without we have the same property in as our lives.

Now as society ought properly to be nothing but a mutual agreement among the inhabitants of a country to maintain the natural rights and privileges of one another against all opposers, whether foreign or domestic, it would lead one to expect to find those rights and privileges no further infringed upon among men pretending to be in that state, than necessity absolutely required. I say again, it would lead one to think so. But I am afraid whoever does will be mightily mistaken. However, as the truth here is of much importance to be known, let it be boldly fought out; in order to which it may not be improper to trace the present method of holding land among men in society from its original.

If we look back to the origin of the present nations, we shall see that the land, with all its appurtenances, was claimed by a few, and divided among themselves, in as assured a manner as if they had manufactured it and it had been the work of their own hands; and by being unquestioned, or not called to an account for such usurpations and unjust claims, they fell into a habit of thinking, or, which is the same thing to the rest of mankind, of acting as if the earth was made for or by them, and did not scruple to call it their own property, which they might dispose of without regard to any other living creature in the universe. Accordingly they did so; and no man, more than any other creature, could claim a right to so much as a blade of grass, or a nut or an acorn, a fish or a fowl, or any natural production whatever, though to save his life, without the permission of the pretended proprietor; and not a foot of land, water, rock or heath but was claimed by one or other of those lords; so that all things, men as well as other creatures who lived, were obliged to owe their lives to some or other's property, consequently they like the creatures were claimed, and, certainly as properly as the wood herbs, etc., that were nourished by the soil. And so we find, that whether they lived, multiplied, worked or fought, it was all for their respective lords; and they, God bless them, most graciously accepted of all as their due. For by granting the means of life, they granted the life itself; and of course, they thought they had a right to all the services and advantages that the life or death of the creatures they gave life to could yield.

Thus the title of gods seems suitable enough to such great beings; nor is it to be wondered at that no services could be thought too great by poor dependent needy wretches to such mightly and all-sufficient lords, in whom they seemed to live and move and have their being. Thus were the first landholders usurpers and tyrants; and all who have since possessed their lands, have done so by right of inheritance, purchase, etc., from them; and the present proprietors, like their predecessors, are proud to own it; and like them, too, they exclude all others from the least pretence to their respective properties. And any one of them still can, by laws of their own making, oblige every living creature to remove off his property (which, to the great distress of mankind, is too often put in execution); so of consequence were all the landholders to be of one mind, and determined to take their properties into their own hands, all the rest of mankind might go to heaven if they would, for there would be no place found for them here. Thus men may not live in any part of this world, not even where they are born, but as strangers, and by the permission of the pretender to the property thereof; which permission is, for the most part, paid extravagantly for, though many people are so straitened to pay the present demands, that it is believed if they hold on, there will be few to grant the favour to. And those land-makers, as we shall call them, justify all this by the practice of other manufacturers, who take all they can get for the products of their hands; and because that everyone ought to live by his business as well as he can, and consequently so ought the land-makers. Now, having before supposed it both proved and allowed, that mankind have as equal and just a property in land as they have in liberty, air, or the light and heat of the sun, and having also considered upon what hard conditions they enjoy those common gifts of nature, it is plain they are far from reaping all the advantages from them which they may and ought to expect.

But lest it should be said that a system whereby they may reap more advantages consistent with the nature of society cannot be proposed, I will attempt to show the outlines of such a plan.

Let it be supposed, then, that the whole people in some country, after much reasoning and deliberation, should conclude that every man has an equal property in the land in the neighbourhood where he resides. They therefore resolve that if they live in society together, it shall only be with a view that everyone may reap all the benefits from their natural rights and privileges possible.

Therefore a day appointed on which the inhabitants of each parish meet, in their respective parishes, to take their long-lost rights into possession, and to form themselves into corporations. So then each parish becomes a corporation, and all men who are inhabitants become members or burghers. The land, with all that appertains to it, is in every parish made the property of the corporation or parish, with as ample power to let, repair, or alter all or any part thereof as a lord of the manor enjoys over his lands, houses, etc,; but the power of alienating the least morsel, in any manner, from the parish either at this or any time hereafter is denied. For it is solemnly agreed to, by the whole nation, that a parish that shall either sell or give away any part of its landed property, shall be looked upon with as much horror and detestation, and used by them as if they had sold all their children to be slaves, or massacred them with their own hands. Thus are there no more nor other lands in the whole country than the parishes; and each of them is sovereign lord of its own territories.

Then you may behold the rent which the people have paid into the parish treasuries, employed by each parish in paying the Government its share of the sum which the Parliament or National Congress at any time grants; in maintaining and relieving its own poor, and people out of work; in paying the necessary officers their salaries; in building, repairing, and adorning its houses, bridges, and other structures; in making and maintaining convenient and delightful streets, highways, and passages both for foot and carriages; in making and maintaining canals and other conveniences for trade and navigation; in planting and taking in waste grounds; in providing and keeping up a magazine of ammunition, and all sorts of arms sufficient for all its inhabitants in case of danger from enemies; in premiums for the encouragement of agriculture, or anything else thought worthy of encouragement; and, in a word, in doing whatever the people think proper; and not, as formerly, to support and spread luxury, pride, and all manner of vice. As for corruption in elections, it has now no being or effect among them; all affairs to be determined by voting, either in a full meeting of a parish, its committees, or in the house of representatives, are done by balloting, so that votings or elections among them occasion no animosities, for none need to let another know for which side he votes; all that can be done, therefore, in order to gain a majority of votes for anything, is to make it appear in the best light possibly by speaking or writing. Among them Government does not meddle in every trifle; but on the contrary, allows each parish the power of putting the laws in force in all cases, and does not interfere but when they act manifestly to the prejudice of society and the rights and liberties of mankind, as established in their glorious constitution and laws. For the judgment of a parish may be as much depended upon as that of a House of Lords, because they have as little to fear from speaking or voting according to truth as they.

A certain number of neighbouring parishes, as those in a town or county, have each an equal vote in the election of persons to represent them in Parliament, Senate, or Congress; and each of them pays equally towards their maintenance. They are chosen thus: all the candidates are proposed in every parish on the same day, when the election by balloting immediately proceeds in all the parishes at once, to prevent too great a concourse at one place; and they who are found to have a majority, on a proper survey of the several poll-books, are acknowledged to be their representatives.

A man by dwelling a whole year in any parish, becomes a parishioner or member of its corporation; and retains that privilege till he lives a full year in some other, when he becomes a member in that parish, and immediately loses all his right to the former for ever, unless he choose to go back and recover it by dwelling again a full year there. Thus none can be a member of two parishes at once, and yet a man is always member of one though he move ever so oft.

If in any parish should be dwelling strangers from foreign nations, or people from distant countries who by sickness or other casualties should become so necessitous as to require relief before they have acquired a settlement by dwelling a full year therein; then this parish, as if it were their proper settlement, immediately takes them under its humane protection, and the expenses thus incurred by any parish in providing those not properly their own poor being taken account of, is discounted by the Exchequer out of the first payment made to the State. Thus poor strangers, being the poor of the State, are not looked upon with an envious eye lest they should become burthensome, — neither are the poor harassed about in the extremity of distress, and perhaps in a dying condition, to justify the litigiousness of the parishes.

All the men in every parish, at times of their own choosing, repair together to a field for that purpose, with their officers, arms, banners, and all sorts of martial music, in order to learn or retain the complete art of war; there they become soldiers.

Yet not to molest their neighbours unprovoked, but to be able to defend what none have a right to dispute their title to the enjoyment of; and woe be to them who occasion them to do this, they would use them worse than highwaymen or pirates if they got them in their power.

There is no army kept in pay among them in times of peace, as all have property alike to defend, they are alike ready to run to arms when their country is in danger; and when an army is to be sent abroad, it is soon raised, of ready trained soldiers, either as volunteers or by casting lots in each parish for so many men.

Besides, as each man has a vote in all the affairs of his parish, and for his own sake must wish well to the public, the land is let in very small farms, which makes employment for a greater number of hands, and makes more victualling of all kinds be raised.

There are no tolls or taxes of any kind paid among them by native or foreigner, but the aforesaid rent which every person pays to the parish, according to the quantity, quality, and conveniences of the land, housing, etc., which he occupies in it. The government, poor, roads, etc. etc., as said before, are all maintained by the parishes with the rent; on which account all wares, manufactures, allowable trade employments or actions are entirely duty free. Freedom to do anything whatever cannot there be bought; a thing is either entirely prohibited, as theft or murder; or entirely free to everyone without tax or price, and the rents are still not so high, notwithstanding all that is done with them, as they were formerly for only the maintenance of a few haughty, unthankful landlords. For the government, which may be said to be the greatest mouth, having neither excisemen, customhouse men, collectors, army, pensioners, bribery, nor such like ruination vermin to maintain, is soon satisfied, and moreover there are no more persons employed in offices, either about the government or parishes, than are absolutely necessary; and their salaries are but just sufficient to maintain them suitably to their offices. And, as to the other charges, they are but trifles, and might be increased or diminished at pleasure.

But though the rent, which includes all public burdens, were obliged to be somewhat raised, what then? All nations have a devouring landed interest to support besides those necessary expenses of the public; and they might be raised very high indeed before their burden would be as heavy as that of their neighbours, who pay rent and taxes too. And it surely would be the same for a person in any country to pay for instance an increase of rent if required, as to pay the same sum by little and little on everything he gets. It would certainly save him a great deal of trouble and inconvenience, and Government much expense.

But what makes this prospect yet more glowing is that after this empire of right and reason is thus established, it will stand for ever. Force and corruption attempting its downfall shall equally be baffled, and all other nations, struck with wonder and admiration at its happiness and stability, shall follow the example; and thus the whole earth shall at last be happy and live like brethren.

An Interesting Conversation, between a Gentleman and the Author, on the Subject of the foregoing Lecture

Gent. So I understand you are the Author of this strange Lecture?

Auth. Yes, Sir.

Gent. Well, though I am a friend to the Reformation of the world, I did not expect any one's ideas would have been carried to such extravagant lengths on the subject as your's.

Auth. And I am as strangely puzzled to conceive how any one, not afraid of the freedom of his own thoughts, could stop any thing short of the system there laid down.

Gent. Indeed! But who, pray, among all the Revolutionists in either America, France, or England, or any where else, ever disputed or attempted to invalidate the rights of the landed interest? Or, does Paine, whose publications seem to satisfy the wishes of the most sanguine Reformers, glance in the least on their rights? This is taking too great liberties.

Auth. I cannot help it. I would sooner not think at all, than check my thoughts on a subject so important. — I hate patching and cobling. Let us have a perfect system that will keep itself right, and let us have done; for what is radically wrong must be a continual plague.

But, Sir, why all this anxiety and concern for the interests of landlords? Those who can reward as they can will never want advocates to defend their cause, whether it be good or bad. "Will you plead for Baal? If Baal be a god, let him plead for himself".

The Reformers, of whom you say you are one, indulge themselves in criticising on, and condemning customs and establishments as old and as defensible as the monopoly of land, and think they are only using the Rights of Men: allow me therefore, to take the same liberty with what I think amiss; and let Baal, as I say, plead for himself. So, Sir, your servant, you may dislike my free manner of defending doctrines, which I think of such magnitude.

Gent. Nay, stop a little Sir, you must excuse me. I was only acting in character; you must allow Baal, as you say, to plead for himself, for I being a landlord cannot be expected to lose an estate without some defence; therefore, indulge me with the solution of such difficulties as appear to me in the principles and execution of your plan, that if I am a loser I may be satisfied that the public good absolutely requires it.

You build your system, I observe, on the supposition that men have the same right to property of land as they have to liberty, and the light and heat of the sun, which I grant is a very just position, respecting men in a natural, or in their primeval state; but this antient and universal right is so set aside and disused, that it seems quite forgot and expunged from the catalogue of the Rights of Men; besides, there was nobody found murmuring at the want of it.

Auth. It is, indeed, very amazing, that people should never think more seriously of such an essential and inestimable privilege, considering the many express declarations to that purpose, to be met with both in the scriptures and in the best of prophane authors. Permit me, then, to produce two or three of the most remarkable passages: and first, from Leviticus, Chap.25th.

> "And thou shalt number seven sabbaths of years unto thee, seven times seven years; and the space of the seven sabbaths of years shall be unto thee forty and nine years. Then shalt thou cause the trumpet of the Jubilee to sound, on the tenth day of the seventh month, in the day of atonement shall ye make the trumpet sound throughout all your land. And ye shall hallow the fiftieth year, and proclaim liberty throughout all the land, unto all the inhabitants thereof: It shall be a Jubilee unto you; and ye shall return every man unto his possession, and ye shall return every man unto his family."

And again in the same chapter, it is said,

> "The land shall not be sold for ever; for the land is mine; for ye are strangers and sojourners with me."

Thus you see God Almighty himself is a very notorious leveller, and certainly meant to stir up the people every fiftieth year, to insist upon liberty and equality, or the repossession of their just rights, whether their masters or creditors were agreeable or not, or whether they might deem it seditious or no; and we may suppose that such of the latter as were covetous ungodly men would behave very frowardly, and quit their hold with much reluctance, and would be far from promoting such a revolution.

Then we may be certain that as often as such periodical revolutions happened in favour of the Rights of Man, they must arise from, and were procured by the irresistable importunities of the slaves and landless men.

Thus we find personal liberty and landed property very properly linked together by our all-wise creator, nor is the one of much consequence without the other. Indeed, I think all our landless people had better live in slavery, under humane masters, that would provide them with the necessaries of life, than be turned out of their rights as outcasts upon the face of that earth whereon they must neither feed nor rest.

Well, we have heard what God has said on the subject, let us next hear what man says. Locke, in his treatise of government writes thus:

> "Whether we consider natural reason, which tells us, that men, being once born, have a right to their preservation, and consequently to meat and drink, and such other things as nature affords for their subsistence. Or, revelation, which gives us an account of those grants God made of the world to Adam, and to Noah and his sons; it is very clear that God, as King David says, Psalm 115, 16, has given the earth to the children of men, given it to mankind in common."

Here we find this great man concurring in the same fundamental principles, as we shall likewise Puffendorf, in his Whole Duty of Man, according to the law of nature, where he observes, that

> "As those are the best members of a community, who without any difficulty allow the same things to their neighbour, that themselves require of him, so those are altogether incapable of society, who, setting a high rate on themselves in regard to others, will take upon them to act any thing towards their neighbour, and expect greater deference, and more respect than the rest of mankind; and, in their

intolerant manner, demanding a greater portion unto themselves of those things, to which all men having a common right, they can in reason claim no larger a share than other men: whence this also is an universal duty of the law natural, That no man, who has not a peculiar right, ought to arrogate more to himself than he is ready to allow to his fellows, but that he permit other men to enjoy equal privileges with himself."

Such declarations being frequent in all the best authors, one would think they would rouse the most supine to consider their contemptible and degraded situation, who, from being the rightful lords of the creation, and only a little lower than the angels, and crowned by their maker, with glory and honour, tamely prostrate themselves to the earth, to a state worse than a reptile, for any one that will be insolent enough to pass over.

But, Sir, people never thought it was practicable to enjoy an equal property in land. For the mechanics thought they could not themselves cultivate land if they were possessed of it, and that therefore thousands would be selling their portions to others, which would soon reduce things to the same situation as at present. And besides, they could not be at the trouble, nor put themselves so much out of temper, so as like the Jews, to demand a restitution of the land and an abolition of debts every fiftieth year. No, they would rather sit down contently on their dunghills, under all their affronts, with their wives and children starving about them than give offence to their masters by seditiously claiming their rights as men.

But, by giving the land to the parishes, they will be eased at once of all those troublesome apprehensions; one hearty revolution and one jubilee will do the business for ever: for we find societie once possessed of land do not easily give it up, but are very tenacious of their property of which we have many instances, there hardly being a corporation but what has landed property, and have retained the same for many ages.

So here is a simple, easy, practicable scheme, which people may see realised in every corporate body; wherefore, as people will now think themselves qualified to manage their own estates by the agency of their parish officers, for their own advantage, they must of course think landlords of no more use, and will grow weary of them. The payment of rent to a landlord, will be like giving money to a highwayman, and they will pant to be rid of their insupportable burdens all at once. In short, Sir, when the public machine is thus set a going on nature's principles, like nature itself, it will never err to any great degree, but on the least aberrition immediately rebound back to its just equilibrium.

Gent. But, Sir, I am not so partial to corporation government, but I can see many things amiss in them. There is often much party work, and I am afraid the people at large would reap small benefit from their landed property, as is too much the case in most of the corporations already in being.

Auth. The corporations now in being were established in times of ignorance, when very few were qualified to take cognizance of public affairs, wherefore the mass of the burghers were never suffered in their own persons to make choice of their magistrates or agents, but every company or trade chose an elector, and these were to make a kind of *sham* choice of magistrates and officers, for all this was settled in reality before in the common council; and the same practice to the great ease and content of the sluggish people, is still continued, which I hope you do not think I approve of; for I see no reason why a candidate for a magistracy or other office may not, after proper examination in respect to abilities, be proposed in every distinct company or trade at the same hour, and then in their own persons proceed to election. Candidates would not find it so easy to make a party among the burghers at large, as they do now among a few deputies, electors, or liverymen; but I hope if the people were but once put right (for they never have been so yet) they would be wise enough never to relapse into insignificance again, and find it worth their while to act in person as much as they could, by admitting of no electors or deputies between them and the person or thing to be voted for; for if a parish were found to be too populous to vote conveniently and expeditiously in one place, they would surely have the sense to divide the parish into such a sufficiency of districts or departments as should render business speedy and generally satisfactory.

I should likewise expect that they would have the sense to cause the parish accounts to be minutely stated and printed, at least every quarter; and the national accounts to be in the same manner printed, at least every year. And I should likewise with that the rents or rates might be collected monthly, as the poor rate is now, which, when once paid, would be in full of all demands, both for rent and taxes.

In short, Sir, if I thought the people at large would ever become so despicably destitute of common sense, as to be incapable of conducting such simple transactions with any little accidental variations after being thus fairly put right — I say, instead of exciting my pity as they now do, I would, like their tyrants, hold them in the most sovereign contempt and derision; nay, I would rejoice in seeing them all delivered over to cruel task-masters, planters, negro-drivers, landlords, and all the devils on earth. Moreover, I would endeavour to get into some infernal office myself, and make my thong the most terrible of the terrible.

But I am far from apprehending will ever be the case, for it is impossible for the world to become generally ignorant again, as it was before the art of printing. Knowledge has been constantly encreasing ever since that happy invention, and will infallably continue to do so while the world endures.

Is it not astonishing, Sir, that republicans who long to put the affairs of a nation into the hands of commissioners or delegates, should despair of managing the rents or revenues of a parish in the same popular way? Is national democracy easier than parochial? Or are the pure rights of a man less defensible against landlords, than the rights of society against kings? The landlords are, and always were, the first infringers on the rights of man, and pave the sure way to regal tyranny. If the earth would remain barren and uncultivated, and if men, like brutes, would live in caves rather than build houses, etc., by means of their own agents or commissioners, then by all means let them have landlords. But then I, for my part, as much despair of the management of a nation by delegation, as others do of a parish, and therefore to me, kings seem to be to the full as necessary to a state, as landlords to a parish.

Wherefore in the name of common sense, let us either quietly submit to matters of every description, or manfully aspire after perfect freedom from every imposition. For why should we despair of managing small affairs as well as great.

    Gent. But I am at a great loss to conceive what will become of all the landed people, gentlemen of the law, gentlemens' servants, many artizans and tradesmen, entirely dependent on the nobility and gentry, and also the soldiers, for you intend all your citizens to be soldiers.

    Auth. You will observe, Sir, that I am proceeding in this affair entirely in confidence of the people having common sense, and that they will, when once put right, put their senses forth to use on all occasions; and, I likewise, suppose they may have as much compassion on those affected by the change of affairs, as justice and necessity will admit of. So, in all probability, on that memorable day, that grand jubilee, when every parish, in some country shall take into its possession its indubitable rights, I mean the land with all its appurtenances, as structures, buildings, and fixtures, and mines, woods, waters, etc., contained within itself: I say, though according to right and system they must seize upon these, I expect they would leave every person in possession of his money and moveable effects to dispose of at his pleasure. The quondam landlords might therefore be reasonably expected to subsist comfortably upon these effects, all their lives with economy, I am sure few of the rest of the people would have as much at that day to their share; and as to their children, they would doubtless suit their education to their prospects, which would be no other than to live as sober, industrious citizens, maintained by their own industry. And what should hinder them by trading or farming to encrease their effects under so mild and cherishing a government, as well as others? The same may be said of gentlemen of the law, and other eminent artists or tradesmen, who might suffer by the change; as for the private soldiers and subalterns, I would wish them to be sent every man to his own parish, there to receive his pay for life, and be employed in training his fellow-parishioners; and the general officers, I hope, the government would provide for in like ample manner. And with respect to other individuals, whether servants, mechanics, or revenue officers, who, having no effects accumulated, and might be reduced by any cause whatever, either at this or any future period to require assistance, I hope their respective parishes would prove generous, and sympathizing benefit societies for support of them all, until they could again provide for themselves; and the parishes, no doubt, would contrive to make such persons contribute, if in health, towards the public good by their labours and to this they surely would not object.

Gent. But, friend, what do you expect by all this? Though your scheme should succeed, you cannot expect an estate for your trouble, and both you and your posterity for ever must be content to herd with the common mass, without any hopes of flattering distinction: but if your plan should not succeed, then you must expect a spiteful and powerful opposition in all you go about, from those you are seeking to overthrow.

Mr Paine acts more cautiously, and does not hurt the feelings of any gentleman that is unconnected with government, and so, of course, may retain their good will, notwithstanding all the lengths he goes; and may, even with a good grace, consistent with his reform, enjoy a very handsome estate, and with all his boasted liberty and equality, may roll in his chariot on the labours of his tenants.

Auth. The contempt and ungenerous rebuffs of the opulent I have already pretty well experienced, and do yet expect; but the feelings occasioned by beholding the struggles of temperance, frugality, and industry, after an honest livelihood, which ought to be easily attainable by every one, have always been sufficiently powerful to enable me to despise them. Yes, those sympathetic feelings were impressed deep on my heart, being first excited by the many difficulties my poor parents experienced in providing for, and endeavouring to bring up their numerous family with decency and credit, which I thought very hard, as none could be more temperate, frugal, nor industrious.

I began, Sir, to look round to know the cause of this piercing grievance, and I found thousands rioting in all the abominations of luxury and dissipation, as if there had been no being in heaven or earth but themselves, and as if they had been created for the sole purpose of destroying the fruits of the earth; and again, I beheld myriads in a much worse condition than my own family. Then I began to read, and I found the savages in Greenland, America, and at the Cape of Good Hope, could all by their hunting and fishing procure subsistence for their families. Then I enquired whether men left the rude state of a savage voluntarily for greater comforts in a state of civilisation, or whether they were conquered, and compelled into it for the benefit of their conquerors. My experience compelled me to conclude the latter, for I could observe nothing like the effects of a social compact; wherefore, I concluded that all our boasted civilisation is founded alone on conquest; nor will any men leave their rude state to be treated with contempt, pay rents and taxes, and starve among us. Savages may sometimes suffer want though that is but rare, but the poor tamed wretch drags on a despicable, miserable, and toilsome existence, from generation to generation. This surely looks exceeding bad, that among men in such high refinement and so capable of rendering each other happy, by being reciprocally useful to each other: thousands should nevertheless be in so wretched a state, that savages would not change conditions with them.

Such studies, Sir, as these, were what stirred me up with an irresistible enthusiasm, to lay before the world a plan of society, so consonant to the Rights of Man, that even savages should envy, and wish to become members thereof.

The Marine Republic (1794)

A Certain man having many sons all bred to a seafaring life, was desirous that they should live together in a just, brotherly, and social manner; and that though he wished to encourage individual industry, and improvement in abilities, by providing that every one should reap the fruits of the same, yet was he determined to form their plan of union in such a manner that none, not even their children, should be so depressed as to be excluded from the common benefits of their birthright and of an equal token of the impartial regard of their common parent. Wherefore one day having called his sons together, he addressed them to this effect:

"My dear boys, my behaviour and conduct towards you, has always been such as to convince you, I was strictly, just, and impartial. You were all equally my delight and care in your infancy, you have been equally provided with the means of Education, and with every comfort and convenience. I have shewn no partiality to any, as being older or younger, I have been in all respects your common parent, and I wish you and your children to live together as my common children for ever, for I extend my parental regard to your offspring through every generation — Behold, then, this gallant ship, equipped and provided with everything necessary for sea, her rigging and tackle all of the best materials, and admirably adapted to the ocean you have to occupy; amply provided with stores and provisions for a long voyage, and waiting only for intelligent and skilful agents to conduct her whithersoever they will. You my dear boys, are such agents, sufficiently qualified for the adventurous task. *Accept, then my sons of this my precious gift, but remember, I do not give it to one, or two, or a select few, but to you all, and as many of your posterity as shall sail therein, as a COMMON PROPERTY.* You shall

all be EQUAL OWNERS, and shall share the profits of every voyage equally among you. You shall choose from among yourselves, one fit to be captain, another to be mate, another carpenter, etc., — These officers shall continue in office while you please, and when you please you shall change them for others, that your affairs may be conducted in the best manner possible. At the end of the voyage, or at other stated times agreed upon, you shall settle your accounts; and after paying the captain, the mate, and every other officer and man his wages, according to station and agreement, and all bills for upholding wear and tear, provisions, etc., then the remainder, which is the net profit of the voyage, and which would have been mine had I retained the property of the ship in my own hands, is now *your* common property, and must be shared equally among you all, without respect to any office any one may have held. For as I make you all equal owners, so shall you be equal sharers in the profits of each voyage. You are all equal to me, and you shall be all equal in this respect to each other. Let not the captain, who receives the wages of a captain, or any other officer, who receives the wages of his station, murmur that his brethren before the mast, and receive only the wages of common men, should receive share and share alike with himself of the profits. No my dear children, let no such unjust and unbrotherly grudging ever be found among you.

"Again my sons, as I have been just and impartial to you, be ye the same to *your* children. And when they shall multiply so that you cannot all sail together in the same vessel, provide another ship out of your common profits, for such of yourselves and your sons as shall choose to sail together, which shall be their common property in the same manner as this ship is yours. This do, and live like men and Brethren through all generations. And as a swarm of bees, when grown too numerous for one hive, send off colonies to people new ones, so when the crews of your ships become too numerous, let new ships be built, and manned on the same equitable plan that I have done, and my blessing go with you."

These injunctions were received by the young men with inexpressible joy. And having wrote them, they were called the Constitution of their "MARINE REPUBLIC", and swore to maintain them inviolate to the end of time. Then they choose a captain, and other officers, and proceeded on a trading voyage, and being prosperous they shared very considerable dividends both at the end of this, and many future voyages.

In process of time, however, it so happened that these marine republicans were dissatisfied with the government of the country, in which they resided. Wherefore taking all their families and all their effects on board, they set sail for America, where they expected to see government administered more agreeably to their notions of equality and equity. But a violent storm arising, they were driven far out of their course, and at last arrived at an uninhabited island of a luxurious soil, and an agreeable climate. Here they gladly landed after much danger, and their ship being so much damaged as to be no more fit for sea, they determined to settle on the island. The ship was now broke up, and houses built with the materials, and preparations were made to cultivate the soil, as they must now think of living by gardening and agriculture. But they foresaw that if they did not apply the Marine Constitution, given them by their father, to their landed property, they would soon experience inexpressible inconveniences. They therefore declared the property of the island to be the property of them all collectively in the same manner as the ship had been, and that they ought to share the profits thereof in the same way. The island they named Spensonia, after the name of the ship which their father had given them. They next choose officers to mark out such portions of land, as every person or family desired to occupy, for which they were to receive for the use of the public, a certain rent according to its value. This rent was applied to public uses, or divided among themselves as they thought proper. But in order to keep up the remembrance of their rights, they decreed that they should never fail to share at rent-time, in equal dividend though ever so small, and though public demands should be ever so urgent.

They now spread considerably over the Country, and houses and workshops were built at the public expense. The space inhabited became too extensive for one district, wherefore they divided it into many, and called them parishes. As they had determined, when seeing that every succeeding ship they should build, and man, should, according to their father's maxim, be the property of the crew, so, in conformity therewith, they decreed, that every district or parish which they should people, should be the property of the inhabitants, and the rents and police of the same at their disposal. Thus they live in union and equality on land, as their father intended they should do on sea, and frame and people new parishes, at the public expense, as he designed they should build new ships. A national assembly or congress consisting of delegates from all the parishes, takes care of their national concerns, and defrays the expenses of state, and matters of common utility, by a pound rate from each parish, without any other tax.

Pigs' Meat 2nd Ed. Vol II, pp.68-72

A Further Account of Spensonia (1794)

The continent not being far distant from the Island of Spensonia, produced several interviews between the respective inhabitants, and of course frequent traffickings and dealings, which on the part of the Spensonians, were conducted with the utmost simplicity and good faith. This uprightness gained much on the affections of the Indians, and naturally produced a yet nearer communication. Contrary to expectation, they here saw a people, much superior in the comforts of life, as independent as themselves; and though Christians, without those *odious tyrants* LANDLORDS. "How", said an Indian to a Spensonian, "How is it that you have no Landlords? We never heard that men could be civilised or be Christians, without giving up their common right to the earth, and its natural produce to tyrants, called Landlords. Among such people, according to universal report, the land is claimed by a few individuals, who dispose of it at pleasure, and parcel it out to others for tribute or rent. Many colonies of Christians have established themselves in various parts of America, and carry on here as in their original country, the iniquitous traffic of the soil. They expel, or exterminate us, the natives, because we will not work, or pay rent to them, for living in our own country; neither have these Europeans the common honesty to share equally, among themselves, their unrighteous plunder; but levy rents of each other here, as they do at home. Yes, their religion it seems will not allow of equality of rights. Their God, they tell us, has ordained that there shall be many *sorts and conditions of men,* and that some few shall have the lordship and disposal of the earth, whilst the far greater part must be reduced to supplicate to become their tributaries and vassals. This has always made us hate your God and your religion. Justice being impartiality, partiality must be injustice; and that God, who is so partial, cannot be just; and not being just, cannot be loved. We cannot love injustice, nor the promoters of injustice. Neither can we, free-born Indians, submit to pay homage or rent to any man for leave to dwell on the earth, though he should say that God would have it so. But you say, *you* are Christians, and that you *nevertheless,* have *no* Landlords; but have an equitable way of enjoying the common benefits of this island which you inhabit, and yet preserve to each man his independence! — This is very amazing to me!" The curiosity of this Indian was satisfied; he was made to comprehend the brotherly system, and that the God of Christians was belied by designing priests, colleagued with overbearing knaves; and that he did not approve, but condemned and punished injustice, usurpation and oppression.

The enraptured Indian sighed for the domestic happiness of civilised life, combined with his native independence. He was adopted a citizen, and was happy. Other Indians, heard, saw, and followed the example. The island now became very populous, and highly cultivated, and many villages increased to large towns, adorned with public edifices, and other marks of opulence and refinement. Trade flourished, ships were built, and commerce extended to distant shores its reciprocal blessings.

In this state of prosperity (says the author of this account) did I find this rising colony, when by accident, some years ago, our ship was driven upon this happy island.

I, like the aforesaid Indian, was astonished when I understood their system of Government, and manner of holding landed property. For instead of anarchy, idleness, poverty, and meanness, the natural consequences, as I narrowly thought, of a ridiculous levelling scheme, I saw nothing but order, industry, wealth, and magnificence. So being anxious to know the utmost of this new-fashioned commonwealth, I took occasion to have my doubts resolved by a communicative

Spensonian as follows:-

Author. *And so none, notwithstanding the splendid appearance the Country makes, and the extensive manner in which trade is carried on, have Estates, nor can purchase any?*

Spensonian. No, nor is it likely ever will; nor does the happiness of human life, or business, require any such nefarious traffic.

Author. *Would it not tend to make the people more industrious if they could lay out their riches in possessions?*

Spensonian. If they were more industrious in order to buy land, other people, being reduced to be their tenants, would, through poverty and oppression, be deprived of the means of industry; and by despair, of the incitement to it. Being possessed of landed property, men would cease to be otherwise industrious than in watching their tenants, in order to raise their rents, and infringe their liberties. Their posterity also, would become equally useless except in the same laudable business of oppression. The same pretence, as to objects of industry, might extend to religion, and the persons of men. Why should traffic be denied to monied men in anything capable of being an object of commerce!! But why despair of industry? You see no want of it among us, not yet among the Jews, neither they nor we can buy land; but, on the contrary, you see a general industry, not one idle. Riches, unsupported by an Estate, would soon take wings, if not prevented by industry. But, in your country, Europe (for I know your customs, we came originally from England), what great incitement, pray, can it be to industry, to give the cream of one's endeavours, unthanked to the Landlord? For what Landlord was ever yet thankful for his rents? They think the tenants owe thanks to them for permission to live on their earth forsooth!

"Wi' glooman brow the Laird seeks in his rent,
It's not to gie;
His honour maunna want, he poinds your gear;
Syne driven frae house and hold, where will ye steer?"

Allan Ramsay

Curse them: I never can think of them but with detestation: I can compare them and their castles to nothing but the giants and their castles in romances. Those giants were said to be a terror and destruction to all the people around, so in reality the dukes, lords, and barons of the present day. Therefore, the stories of enormous and tyrannical giants, dwelling in strong castles, which have been thought fabulous, may reasonably be looked upon as disguised truths, and to have been invented as just satires upon great lords. For, if those fabulous monsters were said to eat the people and their children, your real monsters of Landlords, really eat their meat, and the savour out of every enjoyment; reducing them to such misery, that eating their bodies, as the giants did, would be much more beneficent. They toil them to death in their endless drudgery, harass and butcher them in their villainous wars; and drag them from every social connection. These are the monsters, or giants, that the world want to be rid of. The extirpation of these should employ the philanthropic giant-killers, the deliverers of mankind.

Author. *But notwithstanding all your heat against those Landlords, those monsters as you call them, I should like to know why you think they will never get crept in among you, as they have in all other civilised nations?*

Spensonian. Why, you must know, the interest of every individual is so intimately and palpably connected with our present system, that the least innovation would immediately be felt, and, of course, opposed. People are generally very much attached to their landed property, and societies in particular, are very tenacious of such, especially when they, as we do, find daily the benefit thereof. Then can we suppose any would be so hardy as attempt to touch a whole nation in so sensible a part?

Author. *But bribery, my friend, bribery; that is the invincible Leviathan that overturns the rights of mankind. That may get among you, and numbers may be hired to sell the interests of the public, both present and future, for a little present gain, and be ready either to vote or fight against them.*

Spensonian. Well, I will let you see that though you were to bribe the whole nation you could do nothing by voting, and that you must have a very large majority, before you can have any chance by fighting. You must understand we never vote but by ballot, or in a secret manner, either in parochial or parliamentary business. Now suppose you would bribe the whole of the voters in any affair, and I were one of them, I would reason thus with myself: If I vote as I am bribed to do, I must do wrong to the public, whose interest also includes my own, and perhaps the interest likewise of posterity. If there be but one vote against my briber, he may say it is mine; and if I deny it, so may he that gave this vote, and has as good a chance to be believed, there being no witnesses; whereby I will have the mortification to have wronged my country and conscience, without being able to clear myself in your sight. So, in consequence of this reasoning, I would vote against you; and so would every one else from the same consideration. Let us see how this case will stand then? Why you would chide me privately (for you durst not do it publicly) for not voting for you, though hired. I would say, how do you know that? Because, say you, I have not one vote, *(for remember, if you had but one vote, I would lay claim to it,)* and therefore not yours. What, not one vote! I would exclaim. No, not one; say you. Well then, I would answer, I have the comfort to think I am no worse than others: This will teach you to come hither, again to buy votes. Besides, if I had voted for you, others might have claimed, with you, the merit of the deed, while I would have had the whole of the guilt; and, at best, an equal share of the suspicion. So there is an end to your hurting us by voting.

Author. *I am not convinced, that so long as you vote by ballot, or secretly, there does not appear a possibility of hurting you in that quarter. But is it not beneath freemen to vote thus clandestinely, as if afraid to act honestly in the face of the world? Moreover, you lose all the praise of your good deeds, which is a general incitement to worthy actions.*

Spensonian. In your country they vote in the open manner you commend. What is the consequence? Why the Ministry tells you it is necessary to have a majority on their side for the dispatch of business, which amounts to the same thing as pleading for no parliament at all. A majority therefore is procured, in a very honourable way no doubt. The minority not being bought (for a majority is sufficient) take every opportunity to show their importance, by opposing all business indiscriminately, whether right or wrong. Indeed they have often but too much reason to oppose, yet let their harangues be ever so violent, they can never make the majority understand in any other way than the Minister would have them; for they are too fast asleep in the lap of corruption, to regard either their arguments or the praises of their country. Thus you see the weak influence of fame, which you build so much on, even among senators; what strength must it then have among the poor freeholders and burghers, after so glorious an example!

This general corruption, and conflict of interests, furnish endless materials for newspapers, pamphlets, and state cobblers. Thousands of abortive schemes are daily proposed for redressing grievances and mending the constitution; whereas, the shoes were so ill-made at first, are so worn, rotten, and patched already, that they are not worth further trouble or expense, but ought to be thrown to the dunghill; and a new pair should be made neat, tight, and easy, as for the foot of one that loves freedom and ease. Then would your controversies about this, and the other way of cobbling, that continually agitate you, be done away; and you would walk along the rugged and dirty path of life easy and dry-shod.

And now you shall witness with your own eyes, that force is likely to succeed as ill against us as secret corruption. Therefore you must go with me tomorrow, a few miles off, it being a general review day, when the inhabitants of several parishes together are to go through their military exercise, under the eye of a general, provided by the State. Every parish, or ward of a parish, exercise themselves at their own convenience; but two or three times a year, several parishes are assembled together, as I said, to accustom themselves to act in large bodies, as you will see tomorrow.

Accordingly next morning we were roused early by the drums all over the country beating to arms. No man lagged behind that was able to march; but my friend, luckily for me, happened to be lame, yet not so as to prevent his hobbling there to be a spectator. I was a stranger, and therefore had nothing to do with them; and so went with my friend also to look on. The morning was exceedingly fine, the military ground was spacious, and kept always in pasturage for that purpose. The parishes in different liveries, came marching in from every direction, with artillery, banners, and music. Those who had good horses, were horsemen; and formed into troops according to the colour of their horses. The very boys too were furnished with small arms, and classed according to their sizes. It was delightful to behold so many thousand citizen soldiers in arms only of defence; an army of "men, who their duties know, and know their rights; and, knowing, dare maintain". In short, they made a gallant appearance, and every one was adorned with what little ornament his rank and uniform admitted of; as medals received for improvements, public services, etc. Every eye sparkled with delight, and every countenance was expressive of happiness, for this is their most agreeable sport. Emulative obedience to command, and dexterity of action, was every where conspicuous. What contributed much to this, was, that nothing but eminent merit can advance any to be officers, who must pass through every station to the highest, if their merit can carry them so far. They went through their several manoeuvres like veterans, but the boys in particular made a pleasing sight. No play whatever gives them such delight as this military exercise, which they apply to with such diligence, that before they leave school, or are fit for other employments, they are as complete therein as the oldest. For this purpose all due encouragement is given them; a particular instance of which appeared at this time: They made a mock fight with the men and drove them off the ground, which closed the review. Every party then with colours flying as they came, marched to their respective homes, to spend the remainder of the day in festivity and joy.

The merry bells now sounded from every steeple. The glad females, after feasting their manly spouses and paramours, prepared for the dance; and though the evening, revelled in pleasures known to love and innocence alone. Among other sports, there were shooting matches and cudgel playing, which are favourite diversions, and encouraged, on such days as this, by medals from the parishes. The victors are very proud of these medals, and, as observed before, wear them on extraordinary occasions and field days.

I can never enough admire the beauty of the country. It has more the air of a garden, or rather a paradise than a general country scene; and indeed it is only a continuation of gardens and orchards. For besides the infinite number of real gardens, the very fields, meadows and pastures, are plentifully strewed with fruit trees, and the corn is cultivated in rows, and as carefully as garden herbs. The houses and everything about them are so amiably neat, and so indicative of domestic happiness, so far distant from the inflated pomp and ghastly solemnity of the palaces of the great, and the confined miserable depression of the hovels of the wretched, that they seem the habitations of rational beings; of beings worthy the approbation of the Deity, because, though as he designed them they be lords of all his works, they presume not be Lords of each other.

On expressing my surprise at so much private felicity and public convenience, my friend answered, "The parishes build and repair houses, make roads, plant hedges and trees, and in a word do all the business of a Landlord. And you have seen what sort of Landlords they are. I suppose you do not meet with much to repair or improve. And it is no wonder, for a parish has many heads to contrive what ought to be done. Instead of debating about mending the State, as with you, (for ours needs no mending) we employ our ingenuity nearer home, and the result of our debates are in every parish, how we shall work such a mine, make such a river navigable, drain such a fen, or improve such a waste. These things we are all immediately interested in, and have each a vote in executing; and thus we are not mere spectators in the world, but as all men ought to be, actors, and that only for our own benefit".

The next day following we commenced again our political conversation, as follows:-

Spensonian. Now our whole country is trained and peopled as you have seen, I therefore suppose you have dropped all hopes of fighting us out of our Liberties, and if there were a possibility of voting them away, we would not nevertheless part with them. Nay, we will not suffer, any Law in the least impolitic, to give us uneasiness long; for we are too knowing and too powerful to be imposed upon or brow-beat; which makes our Parliament very careful how they make Laws.

Author. *I must indeed own that you have no great reason to be afraid of any encroachment on your Constitution, whilst you continue your two Guardian Angels; I mean VOTING BY BALLOT and THE UNIVERSAL USE OF ARMS. But I beg the same liberty to make objections that my countrymen will be apt to take when I inform them of your uncommon customs, that I may be the more enable to answer them. Do not people repine that the place they occupy is not their own; that they must pay rent; that they cannot do with it what they please; and that they cannot enfeoff their posterity with the improvements they may make?*

Spensonian. So you think that the unreasoning desires of wayward individuals should be complied with, to the detriment of the whole people? Private property in land, is either just, according to the law of nature, or it is not. That it is not, is evident from the unnatural and oppressive consequences flowing from it. If all tyranny, and abuses in government, flow only from that monopolising system, it must, of course, be the fountain head of tyranny; search history, and see, that the government of every country ever was, and is, in the proprietors of land. If then the people wish to have the government in their own hands, they must begin first, by taking the land into their own hands.

Who is the Lord Paramount of the universe? Is he not God? He then, and he alone or those whom he deputes, must have the rents. Now the Scripture says, that he has given the earth to the children of men; given it to mankind in common. The mankind in their respective districts are his substitutes and representatives, and have a right to receive, and dispose of the revenues arising from the Domains, which he in his providence permits them severally to possess. Some will say, that though God gave the earth to the children of men, in common, they may have private possessions. I answer, yes; if they live far, I mean *very far*, asunder. But in no populous country, since the beginning of the world, was private property in land enjoyed, but to the detriment of multitudes of the same community: Suppose a populous country were divided equally among the inhabitants, as was the land of Canaan among the Israelites, how long would their shares continue equal? In a few years some men's families would increase and others decrease, which would soon produce inequality of estates, even though neither the right of primogeniture nor alienation of property were allowed. Those who became heirs to those decreased families, would become richer; and those who had but a small share among many brethren, of their paternal inheritance would become poorer, and even a periodical jubilee would not prevent injustice and inequality. But, by sharing the rents, man's equal rights and dignity is preserved, in every generation, and in every state of population. If God be just he must approve of so just and impartial a system. We presume that he is so, and that he is not displeased at his revenues, being disposed of so much to the happiness of mankind.

We then admit that of ONE LORD, as we do of ONE GOD, and in his name our rents are collected and disposed of as we believe, according to his will and pleasure. We do not murmur, as you suppose, at paying rent: How should we, when we consider for whose use it is? Does not the rent paid here, serve instead of taxes and rates of every description and is it not wholly at our own disposal? And when the public establishments are provided for, is not the remainder divided equally among us? If when premises become vacant by death, or otherwise, they be let to the best bidder; is not that the fairest way? It shews no partiality and prevents collusion to the prejudice of the public.

And do you think that the people, while a man lives and pays his rent, will be so ungenerous as to turn him out of his house or farm? No – To prevent families indeed, from looking on their tenements as hereditary, the public may think it prudent, at the decease of a man, or his widow, to take again their property into their own hands, and dispose of it again to the best bidder. And what just reasons will the sons have to complain? Are they not part of that public, whose interest every man ought to promote and be jealous of for his own sake? But to prevent all colour of injustice, on account of improvements, medals and premiums are always bestowed on those, while they live, who remarkably improve the public property. Your European landlords give no such rewards, nor shew such favour, on account of improvements, that you need to surmise so many idle grievances under a system of purity sufficient for the heavens.

I could not, in my heart, tease my friend any further, with my frivolous objections; for I was fully convinced that, if ever there be a millennium or heaven upon earth, it can only exist under the *benign* SYSTEM OF SPENSONIA.

The wise and beneficent regulations and laws emanating from this system of simplicity are beyond conception, beautiful and conducive of public happiness. Many instances might be given, which, other societies, not built on the public good, can never adapt. For example: If any man possess an invention, or secret, in medicine, or other science, or art, or importance to mankind, the state does not first tax the possessor by selling him a patent, and then load his manufactures with stamps and duties, thereby counteracting as much as possible, the kind intentions of the deity, in blessing his creatures with such an invention. No: the parliament is *obliged* to purchase the secret, and publish it. Remember, I say *obliged*; for as it is only for purposes evidently useful, that their government dare dispose of the public money, at all, so neither dare they be sparing, when public utility demands it. Thus no quacks or impostors, under pretence of secrets, are suffered to impose on mankind, to ruin their healths, or pick their pockets. Neither does any complain, that his inventions, or his labours have been unrewarded through all the *happy regions* of SPENSONIA.

Pig's Meat 2nd. Ed. Vol.II, pp.205-218.

The End of Oppression (1795)

Young Man. I hear there is another RIGHTS OF MAN by *Spence,* that goes farther than *Paine's.*

Old M. Yet it goes no farther than it ought.

Y.M. I understand it suffers *no* private Property in Land, but gives it all to the Parishes.

O.M. In so doing it does right, the earth was not made for Individuals.

Y.M. But people of all conditions have been so accustomed to think that the completion of all earthly felicity consists in the possession of Landed Property, that it is not likely they will generally be brought to give up the darling hopes of one time or other possessing a snug Estate.

O.M. It is true, if there were no injustice attending the state of a Landlord, it is the most desirable and enviable state in the world, even infinitely more so than that of a King, or any Placeman or Pensioner whatsoever.

Y.M. It is indeed. Every body knows that well. For the Landlord is entirely supreme, independent, and arbitrary, in his own Domains, hence the title *Lord,* and nothing binds him but his *own* Leases, which he for his *own* interest grants. He is in *no* danger of losing his revenues, for he pays himself in a most haughty and lordly manner, without process, and without hardly condescending to ask. And when his rents are brought to him on the very hour they are due, his Dignity will not permit him to be thankful.

O.M. Why, I find you are at least half a Spensonian: You understand something of the nature of the enemy: and I dare say we shall not differ much in opinion.

Y.M. I have heard, read, and seen enough of their oppressions to make me wish them at an end, if possible.

O.M. Whether it be possible we shall see by and by. But for the reasons before-mentioned, unless it be necessary that there should be in a State Freemen and Slaves, *lordly* Men, and *mean* Men, Landlords cannot be suffered.

Y.M. But most people believe it would be unjust to deprive Landed Men of their Property, as many of them have purchased their Estates.

O.M. Landed Property always was originally acquired, either by conquest or encroachment on the common Property of Mankind. And as those public Robbers did never show any degree of conscience or moderation and enslaved for ages, should in the day of reclamation, through an effeminate and foolish tenderness, neglect the precious opportunity of recovering at once the *whole* of their Rights.

Y.M. But I am speaking of the seeming hardships of depriving modern Purchasers of their Property.

O.M. Those modern Purchasers are not ignorant of the manner in which Landed Property was originally obtained, neither are they sorry for it, nor for any other imposition by which they can get Revenue. And every one knows that buying stolen Goods is as bad as stealing.

Y.M. You are entirely right. The conduct of our rich Men is not such as to create much respect for their Property. The whole of their study is to create Monopolies and to raise Rents and Revenues; and, like the Grave, their endless cry is, Give! Give!

O.M. And what was originally obtained by the Sword, they determine to detain by the Sword. Are not they and their Minions now in Arms under the name of Yeomanry, Volunteers etc? And what means the inveterate War commenced by the Aristocracy of the World against France? They know that Mankind once enlightened will not brook their lordliness, nor be content with their Rights by piece-meal; therefore they exert every nerve to prevent light from spreading, and the union of the People.

Y.M. Indeed there cannot be any thing said for them. They

exhibit to us too plainly all the properties and practices of Robbers. Plunder, spoil and contributions they will at all events have though their ill-gotten Lands should swim with blood; fully declaring themselves the true Heirs and Successors of the ancient Nimrods from whom they hold.

O.M. Then let all Men say, Spence has done right in rooting up such a combination of Spoilers, and setting the world free from all exactions, imposts, and abuses, at once and for ever.

Y.M. It is amazing that Paine and the other Democrats should level all their Artillery at Kings, without striking like Spence at this root of every abuse and of every grievance.

O.M. The reason is evident: They have no chance of being Kings; but many of them are already, and the rest foolishly and wickedly hope to be sometime or other Landlords, lesser or greater.

Y.M. But do you think Mankind will ever enjoy any tolerable degree of Liberty and Felicity, by having a Reform in Parliament, if Landlords be still suffered to remain?

O.M. You should first ask if the Landed Interest will let you have a reform, which they will take care to prevent. For a Convention or Parliament of the People would be at eternal War with the Aristocracy. But granting they should so far forget their interest, they would soon recollect their mistake, and set about their true interest again, which is to counteract every species of public good. And full well are they furnished with every requisite for the diabolical Work. The perpetual influx of wealth by their Rents without toil or study, leaves them at full Liberty and Leisure to plot, and supplies them also with the means of fighting successfully against the interests of the working part of the Community, and turn their labours to their own advantage.

Y.M. Yes, it is natural to expect that whether in the legislature or out of it, their whole study will be under every kind of Government, to encrease the prices of what their Estates produce, that their rents may rise. What shall we then account such a body of People, whose interests are only their own, and so opposite to all others, but a public Enemy, a Banditti that must always be watched and sometimes resisted.

O.M. There you are wrong with your watching and resisting.

Who is to watch and resist? Must not all the rest of the world do something for their Bread? And are they not disarmed by the Game Laws, awed by the Military, and by Monopolies, State Tricks, Rents and Taxes reduced to continual Drudgery and Starvation? How many days do you think such a brood of Beggars could maintain themselves in a state of Insurrection against their Oppressors? They must away to their work again. The cries of the famished Families break up their Campaigns before they are well begun, and they must again return to the yoke, like other starved animals, for mere subsistence.

Y.M. O hopeless state of Mankind!

O.M. No, it is not yet hopeless, though the enemy like a numerous Army, be garrisoned and quartered every where among us, and have all the strong Holds, all the Arms, and every advantage that triumphant and cruel Invaders could wish for, yet will a true and universal knowledge of Spence's plain and simple System overturn them, and sweep all their Greatness and Lordliness away in one Day, and leave the world in perpetual and perfect Peace.

Y.M. Some seem to apprehend the mismanagement of the Parish Revenues, and so discourage People from thinking of that System.

O.M. That is the natural work of the Enemy, and must be expected. But it does not become Democrats to doubt concerning it. For if Men cannot manage the Revenues and affairs of a Parish, what must they do with a State? It is almost as absurd to answer such quibbles as to make them. How strange that Men will turn the world upside down to get the management of a Nation, and yet pretend to despair concerning a Parish!!! It is too bad. The villainy is too barefaced. I am weary with combatting the vile sophistry of Scoundrels that are Oppressors, and of Scoundrels that would be Oppressors. But in Spence's Pigs' Meat, you will find the Parish System represented in such a variety of ways, and so plainly evidencing to every Reader, the easy and practicable transition from this scene of Oppression and Woe, to perfect Freedom and Felicity, that I must refer you to that incomparable Work for complete satisfaction on the Subject.

Y.M. I thank you. I will take the first opportunity of

perusing that excellent Book. But in the mean time, for the sake of conversation, let us suppose that a whole Nation no matter whether America, France, Holland, or any other, but as to England, it is entirely out of the Question, were fully convinced of the excellence of this System, and universally wishing its establishment, I should be glad to know the most easy method of doing so, and with least bloodshed.

O.M. In a Country so prepared, let us suppose a few Thousands of hearty determined Fellows well armed and appointed with Officers, and having a Committee of honest, firm, and intelligent Men to act as a provisionary Government, and to direct their Actions to the proper Object. If this Committee published a Manifesto or Proclamation, directing the People in every Parish to take, on receipt thereof, immediate possession of the whole Landed Property within their district, appointing a Committee to take charge of the same, in the name and for the use of the Inhabitants; and that every Landholder should immediately, on pain of Confiscation and Imprisonment, deliver to the said parochial Committee, all Writings and Documents relating to their Estates, that they might immediately be burnt; and that they should likewise disgorge at the same time into the Hands of the said Committee, the last payments received from their tenants, in order to create a parochial Fund for immediate use, without calling upon the exhausted People. If this Proclamation was generally attended to, the business was settled at once; but if the Aristocracy arose to contend the matter, let the People be firm and desperate, destroying them Root and Branch, and strengthening their Hands by the rich Confiscations. Thus the War would be carried on at the expence of the wealthy enemy, and the Soldiers of Liberty beside the hope of sharing in the future felicity of the country, being well paid, would be steady and bold. And wherever the Lands were taken possession of by the People, (which by all means should be as early accomplished as possible) the grand resource of the Aristocracy, the Rents, would be cut off, which would soon reduce them to Reason, and they would become as harmless as other men.

Y.M. If People could but thus become honest and wise

enough to cut off at once the resources of the enemy, they might soon get rid of Oppression. But it is a pity they do not perceive the immediate and inexpressible blessings that would infallably result from such a Revolution.

O.M. The good Effects of such a charge, would be more exhilirating and reviving to the hunger-bitten and despairing Children of Oppression, than a benign and sudden Spring to the frost-bitten Earth, after a long and severe Winter. Only think of the many millions of Rents that are now paid to those self-created Nephews of God Almighty, the Landed Interest, which is literally paid for nothing but to create Masters. — I say only think of all this Money, circulating among the People, and there promoting Industry and Happiness, and all the arts and callings useful in Society; would not the change be unspeakable? This would neither be a barren Revolution of mere unproductive Rights, such as many contend for, nor yet a glut of sudden and temporary Wealth as if acquired by conquest; but a continual flow of permanent Wealth established by a System of Truth and Justice, and guaranteed by the interest of every Man, Woman, and Child in the Nation. The Government also of such a People could no longer be oppressive. The democratic Parishes would take care how they suffered their Money to be lavished away upon State speculations. And their Senators, who could not be Men of landed Property, would be found to be much more honest and true to the services of their Constituents than our now-a-days so much boasted Gentlemen of independent Fortunes.

When a People create Landlords, they create a numerous host of hereditary Tyrants and Oppressors, who not content with their Lordly Revenues of Rents, seize also upon the Government, and parcel it out among themselves, and take as enormous salaries for the Places they occupy therein, as if they were poor Men; so that the Rents which the foolish People foolishly pay for nothing, and the poor dull Ass the Public, become thus loaded, as it were, with two pair of Panyers. So then, whoever will be so silly good-natured and over-generous as to pay Rents to a set of Individuals, must not be surprised, if their Masters by all ways and means and pretences should keep them to it, and give Scope sufficient to their liberal propensities.

FINIS.

Hark! how the Trumpet's Sound......

A SONG, *to be Sung at the End of Oppression, or the Commencement of the political Millennium, when there shall be neither Lord nor Landlords, but God and Man will be all in all.*

First printed in the Year 1782.

Tune — "God save the King"

1
HARK! how the Trumpet's sound*
   Proclaims the Land around
      The Jubilee!
Tells all the poor oppress'd,
No more they shall be cess'd,
Nor Landlords more molest
      Their Property.

2
Rents t' ourselves now we pay,
Dreading no Quarter Day,
      Fraught with distress.
Welcome that day draws near,
For then our Rents we share,**
Earth's rightful Lords we are
      Ordain'd for this.

3
How hath th' oppressor ceas'd,***
And all the world releas'd
      From Misery!
The Fir-trees all rejoice,
And Cedars lift their voice,
Ceas'd now the FELLERS' noise,
      Long rais'd by thee.

4
The Sceptre now is broke,
Which with continual stroke
    The Nations smote!
Hell from beneath doth rise,
To meet thy lofty Eyes,
From the most pompous size,
    How brought to nought!

5
Since then this Jubilee
Sets all at Liberty,
    Let us be glad.
Behond each Man return
To his Right and his own,
No more like Doves to mourn
    By Landlords sad!

  *   See Leviticus, Chap.25.
**   Though the Inhabitants in every District or Parish in the world (except in England have an undoubted right to divide the *whole* of the Rents equally among them, and suffer the State and all public affairs to be supported by Taxes as usual; yet from the numerous evils and restraints attending Revenue Laws, and the number of Collectors, Informers, etc., appendant on the same, it is supposed, they would rather prefer, That after the whole amount of the rents are collected in a Parish from every person, according to the full value of the Premises which they occupy, so much per Pound, according to Act of Parliament, should be set apart for support of the State instead of all Taxes; that another sum should next be deducted for support of the Parish establishment, instead of Tolls, Tythes, Rates, Cesses etc., and that after these important matters were provided for, the remainder of the Money should be equally divided among all the settled Inhabitants, whether Poor or Rich.
***   Isaiah, Chap.14.

A Letter from Ralph Hodge, to his cousin Thomas Bull (1795)

DEAR COUSIN,

I am informed by some of our Neighbours, who have been at town lately, that you are terribly afraid of loosing your *situation*, by a Reform in Parliament, which the Nation is earnestly seeking after. They did not indeed tell me what kind of a *situation* it was that you were in, whether it was in one of the Police-Offices as a runner; in some of the prisons or goals, as a turnkey; in some of the churches, as a beadle, or grave-digger; or whether you were a door-keeper, or ticket-porter, about the treasury; or some other of the public-offices. It is, however, inmaterial what your *situation* is, I only intend to shew that you have less to fear from a Reform in Parliament, than you imagine. But in order to do this effectually, and put things on a right footing, I must beg leave to remind you of your prior *situation* in the country, together with the causes of your present elevation.

Well then, you know Tom, you were a poor Blacksmith, and worked early and late to support a wife, and a large family of children. This you used to do chearfully enough, and was able to make ends meet, keep a little stock of iron, and could spend a social penny, either at wake, fair, or market, like another man, before our rich neighbours took it into their heads to inclose our common. Then it was that you and I, and many more poor people found a great alteration. We could neither keep cow, nor sheep, nor geese as before. Every thing now depended on the ready penny, and to crown our misery, every opportunity was taken to raise our rents, and lower our wages. You know Tom, there was an universal murmuring and discontent through the parish, and you complained as loud as any. The end of the matter was, you know, that the people rose one night, pulled down the fences, and committed some other outrages. — You and some others were taken; you turned informer and every spirited man in the village was transported. You could no longer remain in the country, and the Esquire in regard of your services, procured you your present *situation.*

This is the honourable cause of your promotion, and it is thus, that most *situations* are acquired. It is thus, that the venal drink the tears of the virtuous; and it is thus, that the treachery of a few, rivet the chains of mankind!

However, I am told that you feel much remorse, and that you have sense enough to see that much is wrong; that things are very dear; that taxes grow enormous; that the national debt increases rapidly, and will never be paid. Yes, Thomas, it is this system of running the nation in debt upon every frivolous occasion that will be the overthrow of many *situations.* It will be impossible to bear it long. The interest already is more than the current expences of even our present extravagant government, so that in fact we have two governments to maintain. But if government could be administered at half the present expence (as some think) then have we four governments to maintain.

What will be the end of all this extravagance, no man is allowed to conjecture. But the same system of reciprocal recommendation to better situations, runs through every department of government still, as it has ever done since the commencement of the funding system which has brought us to our present embarrassed state.

Every paltry account of every paltry action is stuffed with encomiums, and suitable *situations* and *pensions,* must of course be provided for every hero, and for every loyal and zealous supporter of the present high *situations.*

Thus all situations hang together, supporting and advancing each other, till they become unsupportable, and till the poor dumb ass on which they ride fall down, unable longer to bear such a cluster of villainy!

But I am apt to believe, that your *situation* Thomas, is not near so good nor happy now, as it was in the country, when you had your cow, and your sheep, and your geese, etc. You had then but little occasion for money. You had little rent, and little taxes to pay. You could speak like an honest man what you thought without fear of loosing your *situation.*

The dread of bringing up children for the army or the town, did not then perplex you. You expected they would be happy cottagers like yourself, and that honesty and industry might always live.

Vain expectations all! We have lived Thomas to see the end of those halcyon days. Great landlords, and great farmers, now engross all the country, and these employ none but great tradesmen. No little masters to be seen now, no medium; but very great, and very little; very rich, and very poor. The country shines with the palaces of placemen and stockholders, or frowns and glooms with goals and barracks; while the poor peasant and mechanic deprived of daily employment, is driven reluctantly to take up his melancholy abode in one or the other. — Sad alternative!

But every extreme works its own cure, and when things come to the worst, they must mend. The national debt, which, to make comfortable *situations,* is so courteously and politely encreased, will be the salvation of this country. Our vessel is now driven among such rocks and shoals, that she must have skilful pilots, or perish. And if the latter should happen we must all get to shore Tom, as well as we can. But woe be to insolent boatswains and blood-sucking pursers then!

Pray then cousin, let me hear of no more foolish ravings about your paltry *situation.* Become a man as before, and if you dare not say in your *situation,* that BLACK is *black,* and WHITE *white,* you may surely at least hold your peace, and cease meanly to assent to and assert falsehoods. Do not despair about a *situation.* If ever a Reform in Parliament take place, which circumstances render inevitable, no person in such *situations* as yours Thomas, will have reason to complain. A parliament that could feel for the *situation* of the nation at large, would both provide adequately for those they retained in *situations* under government, and those whom through motives of economy they discharged. If taxes were less, living easy, and employment certain, it would make the *situation* of every honest man better. Seventeen or eighteen millions a year of revenue, might if properly dealt make a great many comfortable *situations*. A nation, Thomas, that can support a world in arms and in the arts of destruction, could surely at less expence, make comfortable the situations of its own citizens in the habits of peace and industry.

Cease then dear Thomas to be longer the tool of those in higher *situations*, and do not bother, or teaze your poor brother John, with any more letters about religion, or government, or French, or politics. Bless you he don't understand these things, it is only worrying him to no purpose, putting him out of temper, and pushing him into broils, for like all fools, he is fond of fighting about what he does not comprehend.

When those sly foxes above you, make you afraid of your *situation*, they do so only through fear of their own, which are much more valuable, and if there were any danger to arise, they would be sure to place you between them, and it, and moreover, if their *situations* were no better than yours, they would see them at the devil before they would make such a damn'd fuss about them.

Finally then dear cousin, though you got your *situation* rather dishonourably, let it not be retained so. As the apostle says, *let him that stole, steal no more.* Let the sentiments of the country take their course. They never will be driven to believe that black and white is not black and white. They know THE NATIONAL DEBT WILL NEVER BE PAID, and some *begin to shrug about the interest.* Many things else, likewise people know, but I hope they will never know that men of scurvy and starving *situations*, will foolishly endeavour to put out the eyes of their friends. I hope those who have got *situations* of *six-pence, eight-pence* or even a *shilling a day,* will not think themselves so far elevated above their countrymen, as to think their interests separated. They ought to consider that their *situations* may (like those of too many of their own wretched kinsmen and relatives) admit of much improvement, and can hardly be worse. Then, Thomas, I conclude in wishing heartily, with all your old neighbours in the country, for a speedy reform in parliament, and a repossession of our former common.*

I remain your Affectionate Cousin,
RALPH HODGE.

P.S. Our Cousin Parson Bull, is to preach next Sunday from the following words, in the xxii chap of Numbers. *And the Ass said unto Balaam, What have I done unto thee, that thou hast smitten me these three times? — Am not I thine ASS, upon which thou hast ridden ever since I was thine, unto this day; was I ever wont to do so unto thee? And Balaam said, Nay.*

---

* In defence of dividing commons it is alledged that land in a state of inclosure and tillage, is of more advantage to the community at large. Very true; it is so. But why should the poor alone be robbed for the public good? If the welfare of the community require tillage and inclosure, let those who have the right to the common, share the rent of the same, when it is enclosed. If you say for how long? I say for ever. For while the right to the common remains, the right to the produce, or rent remains also. For no generation has a right to sell and squander away the rights of future generations.

The National Debt

For poor Johnny Bull,
Who is now so dull;
A few plain questions,
To suit his thick skull.

QUESTION. What is the national debt?

ANSWER. Money borrowed, by the rich men of the nation, from the rich men of the nation, and placed to the nation's account.

Q. What is done with the money thus borrowed in the nation's name?

A. The rich men of the nation, give it to each other, under pretence of places and services, civil, ecclesiastical, and military.

Q. Are not those places and services, absolutely and indispensibly necessary to the good of the nation?

A. So far the reverse, that many of those places are fictitious and therefore called *sinecure*; but almost the whole are created under the specious but false pretence of war, religion, and jurisprudence, as a colour for distributing the public money among themselves.

Q. Is public money never given but under pretence of some place or service, real or nominal?

A. It is frequently given under pretence of *former* services; and frequently also under pretence of *secret* services; and the sums thus disposed of, are called *pensions*.

Q. Do the rich men make the nation pay interest for the money they thus squander away among themselves?

A. Yes, certainly; for if they alone had it to pay, they would not be so ready at borrowing.

Q. Was it always the custom of those at the head of the nation to govern, by running it in debt?

A. No: Until our glorious revolution, our government, however covetous, or extravagant, never expected more than could be raised upon the spur of the occasion. They had no notion of taxing future generations before they were born.

Q. Is it probable that this system of taxing futurity can continue long?

A. No. For the interest of the debt, will soon be more than the revenue of the country will pay.

Q. How must the interest then be paid?

A. The rich men of the nation, must borrow of each other to pay the interest, as they did before, to fund the principle.

Q. But when the revenue, and the money borrowed, are condemned before hand to pay the interest of the national debt, what must support the government?

A. Those who have got both principle and interest, must then govern gratis.

Q. Will those who have all along paid themselves so liberally, take the trouble at last of governing us for nothing? Surely no. We must inevitably be ungoverned! Can no way be thought of supporting our government in such unparalelled distress?

A. Let them go a pirating with the Algirines.

Q. Nay; them they have long been in league with, and far excelled in depredation, as the African coast, and both the Indies can woefully witness; insolence and robbery, rapine and murder, have been fully tried in every quarter of the globe.

A. Then damn them. I've done with them!

The Meridian Sun of Liberty (1796)

Preface

Citizen Reader. Pray what is all this you make ado about Landlords, and Tenants, and Parishes? We don't understand you.

Author. That is surprising. I thought I had been very plain. But none are so blind as those who will not see. But the reason why I trouble you with my little publications, is, that I wish to teach you the Rights of Man.

Reader. Rights of Man! What? — Don't we yet know enough of the Rights of Man?

Author. No.

Reader. No! do you say? After all that Paine, Thelwall, and other Philosophers, and the French Republic have taught us, do we not yet know the Rights of Man?

Author. No.

Reader. Does not the whole Rights of Man consist in a fair, equal, and impartial representation of the People in Parliament?

Author. No. Nobody ought to have right of suffrage or representation in a society wherein they have no property. As more are suffered to meddle in the affairs of a benefit society or corporation, but those who are members, by having a property therein, so none have a right to vote or interfere in the affairs of the government of a country who have no right to the soil; because such are and ought to be accounted strangers.

Reader. Do you then account men born in a country as strangers to it, and unworthy of suffrage, that unfortunately may have no title to landed property?

Author. Most certainly I do. Especially such men as being afraid to look their rights in the face, have disfranchised and alienated themselves, by denying and renouncing all claim to the soil of their birth, and profess to be content with the "Rights of property in the fruits of their industry, ingenuity, and good fortune". This is the right to property that a Hottentot, a Chinese, or a native of the Moon may claim among us, as well as you. Wherefore, as you are content with the property of a foreigner, pray do likewise be content with the privileges of a foreigner.

Reader. I tell you, we have a right to universal suffrage, as well as to the fruits of our labour.

Author. And I tell you, that such Lacklanders as you have no right to suffrage at all. For you are to all intent and purposes as much foreigners as the Jews. For if birth gave a title many of them might claim as much as you, having been in the country, and perhaps too through as many generations. So it is not birth but property that gives right of suffrage in a society. Sure you do not, by your suffrages, want to interfere in the estate and properties of other men? You own that the landed interest are the legal proprietors of their estates, and of course, the legal possessors of the fountains of life; and yet, by your universal suffrage, you want to modify to your liking, those very estates which you allow to be private property! — You say that no one has a right to set a price on your labour, yet you want to cramp others in the disposal of what you allow to be as much their right. You say you would abolish the right of primogeniture; you would tax all estates according to their value; prevent the monopoly of farms; abolish the game-laws; and this — and thus — at your whim, you would fashion, reduce, melt and pare down private property, contrary to your own fundamental maxims of right and wrong. Pray be consistent; and let us know, before you begin, where you mean to leave off. If the Rights of Man be definable, as I believe they are, let them be accurately defined, and then let them be sacred. This is the only way to procure unanimity of sentiment, and prevent anarchy. Is it necessary that our rights, like the rainbow, should always recede from us as we advance? And they today to be subject to this decree, and tomorrow to that, as if pleaseth a few of our leading demagogues, who only wish us to know in part, that they may lead us like men upon a secret expedition. Does not this look as if they longed to fish in dark and troubled waters?

Reader. Are we then, because we have no land, to do nothing in our own defence against oppression?

Author. If you don't like the country, and the oppression in it, pray leave it. You have no more right to this country than to any other. While you allow the justice of private property in land, you justify everything the landed interest do, both in their own estates and in the Government, for the country is theirs; and what you call oppression, is only their acting consistently with their interest, and they certainly have a right to govern their own property, and what affects it. So as by your own confession you have neither part nor lot among them, you are of consequence only strangers and sojourners. Wherefore the landed interest act infinitely more consistently is debarring such unprincipled Legislators from interfering among them, than you do in demanding rights which are inexplicable. Noble architects, truly; who would pull down before you know what to build. Who, to serve some temporary purpose, perhaps of plunder, would put all things in a state of requisition, and then suffer matters to end in as much, perhaps more, oppression than they begun. This is not establishing the immoveable Temple of Justice, but erecting the wavering standard of Robbery.

Reader. And pray what do you call the Rights of Man?

Author. Read this Lecture, which I have been publishing in various editions for more than twenty years. There you will see the Whole Rights of Man without reserve. There you will see how far men ought to go in recovering their rights, and where, to a hair's breadth, they ought to stop.

Of kings and courtiers how the fools complain!
Nor blame their word inord'nate love of gain.
None think that while dire landlords they allow,
To kings and knaves they'll still be doom'd to bow.

None think that each by favouring the deceit,
Himself's a foolish party to the cheat.
Few can be landlords; and these very few,
Must, to succeed, their brethren all undo.
Yet each low wretch for lordship fierce does burn,
And longs to act the tyrant in his turn!
Nor longs alone, but hopes before he dies,
To have his rents, and live on tears and sighs!

The Rights of Infants (1797)

Preface*

At last Mr Paine has thought fit to own, with the Psalmist, and with Mr Locke, that "*God hath given the earth to the children of men, given it to mankind in common*".

This is a truth so indisputable, and which I always thought of such vast importance for mankind universally to understand and acknowledge, that I have indefatigably embraced every opportunity, from my youth up, to publish it, together with the most consistent plan that I could form thereon.

I am glad that Mr Paine has, even though late, made this acknowledgement, because his celebrity will procure him many readers, and greatly add both to the investigation of this great fundamental truth, and of such philosophical superstructures as may be built on the same. But as to the plan that he has laid down in his AGRARIAN JUSTICE (where he first acknowledges this principle) it does not appear to me to be in any measure just or satisfactory. The principle is without doubt incomparably grand, and the very first maxim in the law of nature, and in the science of right and wrong, and is fraught with all the blessings that can render mankind happy on earth. But, O dire disappointment! Behold! Mr Paine, instead of erecting on this rock of ages an everlasting Temple of Justice, has erected an execrable fabric of compromissory expendiency, as if in good earnest intended for a Swinish Multitude.

---

* The Rights of Infants was wrote in the latter end of the year 1796, but Paine's Agrarian Justice coming to hand before it was published, the following Strictures, by way of Preface and Appendix, were added.

The poor, beggarly stipends which he would have us to accept of in lieu of our lordly and just pretensions to the soil of our birth, are so contemptible and insulting that I shall leave them to the scorn of every person conscious of the dignity of his nature, not detaining the reader from the perusal of the following little tract on the Rights of Infants, where men who dare contemplate their rights, may see them portrayed boldly at full length.

The more I contemplate human affairs, the more I am convinced that a landed interest is incompatible with the happiness and independence of the world. For as all the rivers run into the sea, and yet the sea is not full, so let there be ever so many sources of wealth, let trade, foreign and domestic, open all their sluices, yet will no other but the landed interest be ultimately the better.

In whatever line of business, or in whatever situation the public observe men thrive, thither every one presses, and in competition bid over each other's head for the houses and shops on the lucky spot, thereby raising the rents till the landlord gets the whole fat of their labours. It is the same in respect to the farms; for if a profitable market, foreign or domestic, spring up for the produce of the earth, then farming will be the rage, and every one will over bid another for farms, till they can hardly live by them. Nay, even abolish the tythes, and the rents of the farms will immediately so advance that the whole advantage shall center in the landlords.

Thus all things work together for good to those who love God, which seems to be fully accomplished in the landed interest, who are the visible elect. Yes, for theirs are all things whether the state, the government or the dignities; the principalities, or the powers. All dominion is rooted and grounded in land, and thence spring every kind of lordship which overtops and choaks all the shrubs and flowers of the forest. But take away those tall, those overbearing aristocratic trees, and then the lowly plants of the soil will have air, will thrive and grow robust. Nevertheless, take care you leave not any roots of those lordly plants in the earth, for though cut down to the stump like Nebuchadnezzar, yet if any vestage of the system remain, any fibre of the accursed roots, though ever so small lie concealed in the soil, they would sprout again and soon recover their pristine vigour, to the overshadowing and destruction of all the undergrowth. Thus do philosophy and the purest philanthropy compel us to eradicate this baneful order from human society.

Whether my plan of enjoying man's rights, which I have been publishing in different ways for more than twenty years, be objectionable or no, it is certain it has never been answered; neither have I seen or heard of any arguments on the subject, but what have only more effectually convinced me that no system can be more universally just even to those it seems most to militate against; more easily established, because it is the interest of every one not to oppose it; nor of course more likely afterwards to be more peaceful and permanent.

If I am wrong, let me be confuted; and if I am not, let mankind for their own sakes, pay attention to what I say. They ought at least to give me credit for my disinterestedness in this scheme, for according to it I can have no private landed estate, no tenants to work for me, nor claim any privilege above my fellow-citizens. Wherefore, before any be so ungenerous as to condemn me as presumptuous, I hope they will candidly weigh my several arguments which they will find in the various little things I have published, which are neither many nor dear, and in the following Rights of Infants.

LONDON, March 19th, 1797.   THO. SPENCE

The Rights of Infants Written in the Latter End of the Year 1796

Open thy mouth for the dumb. Prov.xxxi.8.

"AND pray what are the Rights of Infants?" cry the haughty Aristocracy, sneering and tossing up their noses.

Woman. Ask the she-bears, and every she-monster, and they will tell you what the rights of every species of young are. — They will tell you, in resolute language and actions too, that their rights extend to a full participation of the fruits of the earth. They will tell you, and vindicate it likewise by deeds, that mothers have a right, at the peril of all opposers, to provide from the elements the proper nourishments of their young. And seeing this, shall we be asked what the Rights of Infants are? As if they had no rights? As if they were excrescences and abortions of nature? As if they had not a right to the milk of our breasts? Nor we a right to any food to make milk of? As if they had not a right to good nursing, to cleanliness, to comfortable cloathing and lodging? Villains! Why do you ask that aggravating question? Have not the foxes holes, and the birds of the air nests, and shall the children of men have not where to lay their heads? Have brute-mothers a right to eat grass, and the food they like best, to engender milk in their dugs, for the nourishment of their young and shall the mothers of infants be denied such a right? Is not this earth our common also, as well as it is the common of brutes? May we not eat herbs, berries, or nuts as well as other creatures? Have we not a right to hunt and prowl for prey with she-wolves? And have we not a right to fish with she-otters? Or may we not dig coals or cut wood for fuel? Nay, does nature provide a luxuriant and abundant feast for all her numerous tribes of animals except us? As if sorrow were our portion alone, and as if we and our helpless babes came into this world only to weep over each other?

Aristocracy (sneering). And is your sex also set up for pleaders of rights?

Woman. Yes, Molochs! Our sex were defenders of rights from the beginning. And though men, like other he-brutes, sink calmly into apathy respecting their offspring, you shall find nature, as it never was, so it never shall be extinguished in us. You shall find that we not only know our rights, but have spirit to assert them, to the downfall of you and all tyrants. And since it is so that the men, like he-asses, suffer themselves to be laden with as many pair of panyers of rents, tythes, etc., as your *tender* consciences please to lay upon them, we, even we, the females, will vindicate the rights of the species, and throw you and all your panyers in the dirt.

Aristocracy. So you wish to turn the cultivated world into a wilderness, that you may eat wild fruits and game like Indians?

Woman. No, Sophists, we do not want to be as Indians. But the natural fruits of the earth being the fruits of our undoubted common, we have an indefeasible right to, and we will no longer be deprived of them, without an equivalent.

Aristocracy. Do you not, in lieu of those wild productions, get bread, and mutton, and beef, and garden stuff, and all the refined productions and luxuries of art and labour; what reason then have you to complain?

Woman. Are you serious? Would you really persuade us that we have no reason to complain? Would you make us believe that we receive these productions of art and culture as a fair compensation for the natural produce of our common, which you deprive us of? Have we not to purchase these things before we enjoy them?

Aristocracy. Sure, woman, you do not expect the fruits of men's labours and ingenuity for nothing! Do not the farmers, in the first place, pay very high rents for their farms; and, in the next place, are they not at great trouble and expence in tilling and manuring the ground, and in breeding cattle; and surely you cannot expect that these men will work and toil, and lay out their money for you, for nothing.

Woman. And pray, ladies and gentlemen, who ever dreamt of hurting the farmers, or taking their provisions for nothing, except yourselves? It is only the privileged orders, and their humble imitators on the highway, who have the impudence to deprive men of their labours for nothing. No; if it please your noblenesses and gentlenesses, it is you, and not the farmers, that we have to reckon with. And pray now, your highnesses, who is it that receive those rents which you speak of from the farmers?

Arist. We, to be sure; we receive the rents.

Woman. You, to be sure! Who the D-v-l are you? Who gave you a right to receive the rents of our common?

Arist. Woman! Our fathers either fought for or purchased our estates.

Woman. Well confessed, villains! Now out of your own mouths will I condemn you, you wicked Molochs! And so you have the impudence to own yourselves the cursed brood of ruffians, who by slaughter and oppression, usurped the lordship and dominion of the earth, to the exclusion and starvation of weeping infants and their poor mothers? Or, at the best, the purchasers of those ill-got domains? O worse than Molochs! now let the blood of the millions of innocent babes who have perished through your vile usurpations be upon your murderous heads! You have deprived the mothers of nature's gifts, and farmed them out to farmers, and pocketed the money, as you audaciously confess. Yes, villains! you have treasured up the tears and groans of dumb, helpless, perishing, dying infants. O, you bloody landed interest! you band of robbers! Why do you call yourselves ladies and gentlemen? Why do you assume soft names, you beasts of prey? Too well do your emblazoned arms and escutcheons witness the ferocity of your bloody and barbarous origin! But soon shall those audacious Gothic emblems of rapine cease to offend the eyes of an enlightened people, and no more make an odious distinction between the spoilers and the spoiled. But, ladies and gentlemen, is it necessary, in order that we eat bread and mutton, that the rents should be received by you? Might not the farmers as well pay their rents to us, who are the natural and rightful proprietors? If, for the sake of cultivation, we are content to give up to farmers our wild fruits, our hunting grounds, our fish and game; our coalmines, and our forests, is it not equitable that we should have the rents in lieu thereof? If not, how can the farmers have the face to sell us again the produce of our own land?

Hear me! ye oppressors! ye who live sumptuously every day! ye, for whom the sun seems to shine, and the seasons change, ye for whom alone all human and brute creatures toil, sighing, but in vain, for the crumbs which fall from your overcharged tables; ye, for whom alone the heavens drop fatness, and the earth yields her encrease; hearken to me, I say, ye who are not satisfied with usurping all that nature can yield; ye, who are insatiable as the grave; ye who would deprive every heart of joy but your own, I say hearken to me! Your horrid tyranny, your infanticide is at an end! Your grinding the faces of the poor, and your drinking the blood of infants, is at an end! The groans of the prisons, the groans of the camp, and the groans of the cottage, excited by your infernal policy, are at an end! And behold the whole earth breaks forth into singing at the new creation, at the breaking of the iron rod of aristocratic sway, and at the rising of the everlasting sun of righteousness!

And did you really think, my good gentlefolk, that you were the pillars that upheld the universe? Did you think that we would never have the wit to do without you? Did you conceive that we should never be able to procure bread and beef, and fuel, without your agency? Ah! my dear creatures, the magic spell is broke. Your sorceries, your witchcrafts, your priestcrafts, and all your juggling crafts, are at an end; and the Meridian Sun of Liberty bursts forth upon the astonished world, dispelling the accumulated mists of dreary ages, and leaves us the glorious blue expanse, of serene unclouded reason.

Well then, since you have compelled, since you have driven us, through your cruel bondage, to emancipate ourselves, we will even try to do without you, and deal with the honest farmers ourselves, who will find no difference, unless for the better, between paying their rents to us and to you.

And whereas we have found our husbands, to their indelible shame, woefully negligent and deficient about their own rights, as well as those of their wives and infants, we women, mean to take up the business ourselves, and let us see if any of our husbands dare hinder us. Wherefore, you will find the business much more seriously and effectually managed in our hands than ever it has been yet. You may smile, tyrants, but you have juster cause to weep. For, as nature has implanted into the breasts of all mothers the most pure and unequivocal concern for their young, which no bribes can buy, nor threats annihilate, be assured we will stand true to the interest of our babes, and shame, woe, and destruction be to the pitiful varlet that dare obstruct us. For their sakes we will no longer make brick without straw, but will draw the produce of our estate. If we deprive ourselves of our common, in order that it may be cultivated, we ourselves will have the price thereof, that we may buy therewith, as far as it will go, the farmer's produce. And so far as our respective shares of the rent may be inadequate to the comfortable and elegant support of ourselves and infants, so far will we chearfully, by our honest endeavours, in our several callings, make up the deficiency, and render life worth enjoying. To labour for ourselves and infants we do not decline; but we are sick of labouring for an insatiable aristocracy.

To convince your highnesses that our plan is well digested, I will lay it before you. You will find it very simple, but that is the sign of the greater perfection. As I said before, we women (because the men are not to be depended on) will appoint, in every parish, a committee of our own sex, (which we presume our gallant lock-jawed spouses and paramours will at least, for their own interest, not oppose,) to receive the rents of the houses and lands already tenanted, and also to let, to the best bidders, on seven years leases, such farms and tenements as may, from time to time, become vacant. Out of those rents we can remit to government so much per pound, according to the exigencies of the state, in lieu of all taxes; so that we may no longer have taxes nor tax-gatherers. Out of these rents we shall next pay all our builders and workmen that build or repair our houses; pave, cleanse, or light our streets; pay the salaries of our magistrates and other public officers. And all this we women shall do quarterly, without a bank or bank-notes, in ready money, when the rents are paid in; thus suffering neither state nor parish to run in debt. And as to the overplus, after all public expences are defrayed, we shall divide it fairly and equally among all the living souls in the parish, whether male or female; married or single; legitimate or illegitimate; from a day old to the extremest age; making no distinction between the families of rich farmers and merchants, who pay much rent for their extensive farms or premises, and the families of poor labourers and mechanics, who pay but little for their small apartments, cottages and gardens, but giving to the head of every family a full and equal share for every name under his roof.

And whereas births and funerals, and consequent sicknesses, are attended with expence, it seems requisite to allow, at quarter-day, to the head of every family, a full share for every child that may have been born in his house since the former quarter-day, though the infant may be then but a day old; and also, for every person who may have died since the former quarter-day, though the death should have happened but a day after it.

This surplus, which is to be dealt out again among the living souls in a parish every quarter day, may be reasonably supposed to amount to full two-thirds of the whole sum of rents collected. But whatever it may amount to, such share of the surplus rents is the imprescriptible right of every human being in civilized society, as an equivalent for the natural materials of their common estate, which by letting to rent, for the sake of cultivation and improvement, they are deprived of.

Wherefore, now ladies and gentlemen, you see the glorious work is done! and the rights of the human species built on so broad and solid a basis, that all your malice will not be able to prevail against them! Moreover, when we begin with you, we will make a full end of your power at once. We will not impoliticly tamper with the lion, and pluck out a tooth now and then, as some propose to melt down your strength by degrees, which would only irritate you to oppose us with all the power you had remaining. No; we will begin where we mean to end, by depriving you instantaneously, as by an elective shock, of every species of revenue from lands, which will universally, and at once, be given to the parishes, to be disposed of by and for the use of the inhabitants, as said before.

But yet be not cast down, my good ladies and gentlemen, all this is done for the sake of system, not revenge or retaliation, for we wish not to reduce you to beggary, as you do us, for we will leave you all your moveable riches and wealth, all your gold and silver, your rich clothes and furniture; your corn and cattle, and every thing that does not appertain to the land as a fixture, for these, you know, must come to the parish with our estates. So that you see you will still be the richest part of the community, and may, by your chearful acquiescence, be much more happy than you are now under the existing unjust system of things. But if, by foolish and wicked opposition, you should compel us, in our own defence, to confiscate even your moveables, and perhaps also to cut you off, then let your blood be upon your own heads, for we shall be guiltless. It will therefore be your interest and wisdom to submit peaceably, and fraternize chearfully with us as fellow-citizens. For, instead of you then having the revenues of the country to carry on war against us, as you have now, the parishes will then have these revenues to carry on the war against you. And as to your moveable property, we are not afraid of it, for it would soon melt away in supporting you in a state of hostility against the strength and standing revenues of the country, unburthened with debts and pensions. So prepare yourselves peaceably to acquiesce in the new system of things, which is fast approaching. And when you shall hear of the blessed decree being passed by the people, that the land is from that day forth parochial property, join chorus with your glad fellow-creatures, and joyfully partake in the universal happiness.

The Golden Age, so fam'd by men of yore,
Shall now be counted fabulous no more.
The tyrant lion like an ox shall feed,

And lisping Infants shall tam'd tygers lead:
With deadly asps shall sportive sucklings play,
Nor ought obnoxious blight the blithesome day.
Yes, all that prophets e'er of bliss foretold,
And all that poets ever feign'd of old,
As yielding joy to man, shall now be seen,
And ever flourish like an evergreen.
Then, Mortals, join to hail great Nature's plan,
That fully gives to Babes those Rights it gives to Man.

Chorus. – *To the Tune of "Sally in our Alley".*

Then let us all join heart in hand,
    Through country, town, and city;
Of every sex and every age,
    Young men and maidens pretty.
To haste this Golden Age's reign,
    On every hill and valley,
Then Paradise shall greet our eyes,
    Through every street and alley.

CONCLUSION

BUT stop, don't let us reckon without our host; for Mr Paine will object to such an equal distribution of the rents. For says he, in his Agrarian Justice, the public can claim but a *Tenth Part* of the value of the landed property as it now exists, with its vast improvements of cultivation and building. But why are we to be put off now with but a Tenth Share? Because, says Mr Paine, it has so improved in the hands of private proprietors as to be of ten times the value it was of in its natural state. But may we not ask who improved the land? Did the proprietors alone work and toil at this improvement? And did we labourers and our forefathers stand, like Indians and Hottentots, idle spectators of so much public-spirited industry? I suppose not. Nay, on the contrary, it is evident to the most superficial enquirer that the labouring classes ought principally to be thanked for every improvement.

    Indeed, if there had never been any slaves, any vassals, or any day-labourers employed in building and tillage, then the proprietors might have boasted of having themselves created all this gay scene of things. But the case alters amazingly, when we consider that the earth has been cultivated either by slaves, compelled, like beasts, to labour, or by the indigent objects whom they first exclude from a share in the soil, that want may compel them to sell their labour for daily bread. In short, the great may as well boast of fighting their battles as of cultivating the earth.

The toil of the labouring classes first produces provisions, and then the demand of their families creates a market for them. Therefore it will be found that it is the markets made by the labouring and mechanical tribes that have improved the earth. And once take away these markets, or let all the labouring people, like the Israelites, leave the country in a body, and you would immediately see from what cause the country had been cultivated, and so many goodly towns and villages built.

You may suppose that after the emigration of all these beggarly people, every thing would go on as well as before: that the farmer would continue to plough, and the town landlord to build as formerly. I tell you nay; for the farmer could neither proceed without labourers nor find purchasers for his corn and cattle. It would be just the same with the building landlord, for he could neither procure workmen to build, nor tenants to pay him rent.

Behold then your grand, voluptuous nobility and gentry, the arch cultivators of the earth; obliged, for lack of servants, again to turn Gothic hunters, like their savage forefathers. Behold their palaces, temples, and towns, mouldering into dust, and affording shelter only to wild beasts; and their boasted, cultivated fields and garden, degenerated into a howling wilderness.

Thus we see that the consumption created by the mouths, and the backs, of the poor despised multitude, contributes to the cultivation of the earth, as well as their hands. And it is also the rents that they pay that builds the towns, and not the racking building landlord. Therefore, let us not in weak commiseration be biassed by the pretended philanthropy of the great, to the resignation of our dearest rights. And if our estates have improved in their hands, during their officious guardianship, the D-v-l thank them; for it was done for their own sakes, not for ours, and can be no just bar against us recovering our rights.

APPENDIX

A Contrast between Paine's *Agrarian Justice,* and Spence's *End of Oppression.*

Both being built on the same indisputable principle, viz. that the Land is the common Property of Mankind.

Under the system of Agrarian Justice,	Under the system of the End of Oppression,
The people will, as it were, sell their birth-right for a mess of porridge, by accepting of a paltry consideration in lieu of their rights.	The people will receive, without deduction, the whole produce of their common inheritance.
Under the first, The people will become supine and careless in respect of public affairs, knowing the utmost they can receive of the public money.	Under the second, The people will be vigilant and watchful over the public expenditure, knowing that the more there is saved their dividends will be the larger.
Under the first, The people will be more like pensioned emigrants and French priests than interested natives.	Under the second, The people will be all intent upon the improvement of their respective parishes, for the sake of the increased shares of the revenues, which on that account they will receive.
Under the first, The people cannot derive right of suffrage in national affairs from their compromisory stipends.	Under the second, Universal suffrage will be inseparably attached to the people both in parochial and national affairs, because the revenues both parochial and national will be derived immediately from their common landed property.
Under the first, The government may be either absolute monarchy, aristocracy, democracy or mixed.	Under the second, The government must of necessity be democratic.
Under the first, All the complexities of the present public establishments which support such hosts of placemen, will not only still	Under the second, There can be but two descriptions of public officers, parochial and national, and those but few in number, and on moderate salaries.

continue, but also the evils of them will be greatly enhanced by the very system of Agrarian Justice.

Under the first,
There can exist two spirits, incompatible in a free state, the intolerant and overbearing spirit of aristocracy, and the sneaking unmanly spirit of conscious dependence.

Under the second,
There will exist only the robust spirit of independence, mellowed and tempered by the presence and check of equally independent fellow-citizens.

Under the first,
The destructive profickgacy of the great, and the wretched degeneracy of the poor, will still continue, and will increase, to the pitiable unhappiness of both parties.

Under the second,
All the virtues being the natural offspring of a general and happy mediocrity, will at once step forth into use, and progressively increase their blessed influence among men.

Under the first,
Taxes, both directly and indirectly, will not only be demanded, but will be increased to the utmost the people can possibly bear, let trade and seasons be ever so prosperous.

Under the second,
There can be no taxes, nor expenses for collecting them, because the government would be supported by a poundage from the rents which each parish would send quarterly to the national treasury, free of all expense; thus leaving the price of all commodities unencumbered with any addition but the price of labour.

Under the first,
The poor would still continue, through despair, unambitious to arise out of their hopeless state of abject wretchedness and vulgarity.

Under the second,
The lowest and most profilgate having such frequent opportunities, by the aid of their quarterly dividends, of starting into industrious and decent modes of life, could not always resist the influence of the general virtue every where displayed, without some time or other following the example.

Under the first,
Children will still be considered as grievous burdens in poor families.

Under the second,
As both young and old share equally alike of the parish revenues, children and aged relations living in a family will, especially in rich parishes, where the dividends are

THOMAS SPENCE

Under the first,
If the aristocratic assistance afforded by charity-schools, in the education of poor children be withdrawn, the labouring classes will degenerate into barbarous ignorance.

Under the first,
The poor must still look up for aristocratic benefactions of rotten potatoes and spoiled rice, and other substitutes for bread in the times of scarcity, to preserve their wretched existence.

Under the first,
After admitting that the earth belongs to the people, the people must nevertheless compromise the matter with their Conquerors and oppressors, and still suffer them to remain as a distinct and separate body among them, in full possession of their country.

Under the first,
If foreign and domestic trade increase, the productions of the land will increase in price, of which the landed interest will reap the advantage, by raising the rents in due proportion until the whole benefit thereof centres in them.

Under the first,
All the aristocratic monopolies in trade, in privileges, and government, will continue.

Under the first,
A timid and acquiescing spirit

large, through high rents or the production of mines etc., be accounted as blessings.

Under the second,
If the people are not generally learned it must be their own fault, as their inexhaustible means of comfortable subsistence must furnish also the means of education.

Under the second,
What with the annihilation of taxes and the dividends of the parochial rents, together with the honest guardianship of their popular government, we may reasonably suppose that the people will rarely be driven to the dire necessity of using a substitute for bread.

Under the second,
After insisting that the land is public property, the people's oppressors must either submit to become undistinguishable in the general mass of citizens or fly the country.

Under the second,
If foreign and domestic trade increase, the price of commodities will in proportion also increase, and the rents of course will rise, but this increase will revert back to the body of the people, by increasing their quarterly dividends.

Under the second,
There can be no monopolies; but a fair, salutary, and democratic competition will pervade everything.

Under the second,
The justness and consistency of

must be promoted among the people as now, lest they should discover the dissimilarity between their natural rights and enjoyments.

Under the first,
Domestic trade will be far from its natural height, because multitudes of the people will be poor and beggarly, and unable to purchase numberless articles of use and luxury that their wants and inclinations would prompt them to wish for.

Under the first,
The fund proposed by Paine will require a great number of placemen of various descriptions to manage it, and who being chosen, as they must be, by the ministry and their friends, will very much increase the already enormous influence of governments.

Under the first,
The rich would abolish all hospitals, charitable funds, and parochial provision for the poor, telling them, that they now have all that their great advocate, Paine, demands, as their rights, and what he exultingly deems as amply sufficient to ameliorate their condition and render them happy, by which the latter end of our reformation will be worse than the beginning.

affairs will invite, nay, challenge, the most vigorous and logical enquiries, and will draw forth, uncramped, the utmost powers of the mind.

Under the second,
Domestic trade would be at amazing pitch, because there would be no poor; none but would be well clothed, lodged, and fed: and the whole mass of rents, except a trifle to the government, being circulated at home, in every parish, every quarter, would cause such universal prosperity as would enable every body to purchase not only the necessities of life, but many elegancies and luxuries.

Under the second,
The government can have very little influence by places, because the parish officers will be chosen by the parishioners; and all the complex machinery of financiering and stock-jobbing; all the privileged trading companies and corporate towns, which are the roots of influence and corruption, would be abolished.

Under the second,
The quarterly dividends, together with the abolishment of all taxes, would destroy the necessity of public charities; but if any should be thought necessary, whether to promote learning, or for other purposes, the parochial and national funds would be found at all times more than sufficient.

The Restorer of Society to its Natural State (1803)

Motto — "Schemers of Every Class form an useful Race of Men and are not yet considered as they deserve. The bold political Inovator is probably as necessary a Character as any other for the improvement of the World. He leads us beyond the bounds of Habit and Custom a necessary step to future Advances; and though he may sometimes lead us wrong it is better perhaps to go wrong sometimes than stand still too long.[1]

Preface

Having left the Manuscript of the following Letters with a certain Bookseller for his perusal he lent them to a Friend who wrote some Remarks on them, and though they are sufficiently anticipated and rendered nugatory by what has been advanced both in the said Letters and the other Tracts on the same subject which I have before published, yet as the same Doubts are frequently expressed by other superficial and malignant Examiners it may not be amiss to take some Notice of them.

Objection 1. — "A fine system to establish Civil Wars". If but a few Kings at a great distance from each other are ever and anon at War what may we expect when every Parish proclaims itself Monarch of its soil but every trivial Trespass imagined or real to involve them and their Neighbours in horrid Broils which like a stone thrown into a Pond will undulate the whole mass to its utmost verge.

Answer. — This Gentleman might have reflected that Parishes are too small Communities to wage War on each other, and that in case of Disputes they would be more inclined to submit to the Decision of the Law than the Sword. It is to prevent two powerful associations of Citizens so intimately connected that I propose the Land rather to be parochial property than provincial. Therefore we have nothing to dread from the Disputes of such small Bodies. Besides the Bounds of Parishes have been fixed for so many ages that I cannot perceive how any Difference can arise. Moreover, there would be the National Courts, and the Legislative Body, as well as the Provincial Administrations continually presiding, assisted by all the Wisdom and Precedents of the present and past ages to direct them in every affair.

Objection 2. — "What must those Parishes do who have no Land?"

I answer they must be content with their Lot in that respect as they are forced to be at present. And as Nobody would be bound against their Will to remain always in one Parish, any more then than now, those who wished to change their Residence or Calling would be at Liberty so to do, and might take either Farms in the Country or Buildings in Towns as suited their Inclinations and Business. Such Liberty being granted there could be no cause of complaint concerning the local Advantages of one Parish above another. Besides all Public Burdens being defrayed by an equal Land-tax or Poundage to the State and the County the richest Parishes in Revenue would have to pay most. Wherefore the poorest Parishes might rejoice as well, as the richest at having a public Estate to stand between them and all such heavy Taxes and Enthralments as they now groan under. Thus there would be no Cause for murmuring and envying. The People's good sense, the happiness they would feel, and the Wisdom of the Government for the Time being would always be sufficient to prevent Every Reason of Complaint.

Objection 3. — "Can it be consistent with Justice to plunder any Individual who having perhaps in the Decline of Life expended the whole Produce of his Life in the Purchase of Land for his Subsistence; while those who have no property nor ever worked for it are to have an Equal Share with himself. — And those who have fortunately vested their Earnings in Goods, Merchandise or Cattle are to suffer no Diminution, yet be equal Partakers of the first Man's Land? This would be most horrid Robbery, and most brutally cruel, by reducing a Man infirm to all the Misery of the most indigent without that Health, Strength, or Ability to Endure Hardness which the Laborious Class Enjoy".[2]

There is a feeling Advocate for the Rich! But let us try if we can plead as feelingly for the Poor.

Pray how many have we among the Poor that though they have laboured hard all their Lives and Contributed as much as they could to Enrich and Embellish the World with their useful Works and now in the Decline of Life without Health, Strength or Ability to Endure "Hardness", and have neither Money nor Land, and by no fault of their own too, and yet Nobody pities them? But as none Ever Expend all their Money in Land but reserve sufficient to replenish their spacious and lordly Mansions with Abundance of rich Furniture, Clothes, Jewels, Plate, etc. So those lamented People after their Lands are sequestered will still be the richest, therefore why is all this ado about them? Besides we seldom see People that work hard or get their Earnings laudable buy Land, but rather Monopolisers and Forestallers, Plundering Nabobs, Slave Traders, Corrupt Statesmen, Traitors, and all sorts of Griping Miscreants, who like Judas come with the Reward of Iniquity in their hand to buy a Field of Blood!

But all the Landed People are not fresh Purchasers but rather old Possessors by Inheritance, and have had Time sufficient to fatten on our Property, and therefore have no Reason to complain when we take our own again.

As to saying we are partial to those who have vested their Earnings in Goods, Merchandise or Cattle, it is a mistake, for we have nothing to do with any Thing but the Land, and that is ours both by Justice and Policy. It is ours in Justice, even though we were Brutes, because it is our common Pasture and hunting Park.

And it is ours by Right of Policy, because, by the Aid of it, and the Revenues it produces the Owners are enabled to rule over us, starve us, or do with us what they please. Therefore Necessity which is above all Law, gives us a Right to take so dangerous a Weapon from our Enemies.

Let the delicate Advocates of the Rich read the proceedings of Moses, Lycurgus, and other ancient Lawgivers and see whether they were so tender of what stood in their way. There were Establishments to overturn in their Days as well as the present, yet they did not regard them. And there is no Establishing a regular System without making clear ground to build on and overcoming all Impediments.

But I may desire the Great to look only a little to their own Proceedings and see whether they regard us as our Interest, when they wish to make Laws or Regulations to suit themselves. We must give Way Even before such as their Game Laws that have neither Justice nor Necessity for their plea. But what signifies attempting to specify the numberless Modes in which they treat us with Injury and Contempt. It is impossible. For on our part it is all suffering and on theirs all Insult and Oppression.

Objection 4. – "What Crime has any Man Committed by barely vesting his Property in Lands or in the Funds?"

I answer it was never supposed a Crime while the present System Continues, but it certainly would be a Crime in such a Man, or any Men, to oppose the Extinction of such nefarious Traffic. For like the Slave Trade it is fraught with Every Mischief and Evil to the Human Race, and the same Arguments will serve to defend the one Kind of Traffic as the other. Good God! Is there to be no End or stop to this Traffic? Must nothing be held sacred from Commerce? No! It seems not. But in order to give free Scope to the Speculations of these People of Property all Bounds must be thrown down and Every Thing must be vendable Even to a Porter's place in the Stamp Office. For this very Day, that I am writing this, there is an Advertisement in the public papers offering Fifty Pounds to any Lady or Gentleman, that will procure the Advertiser a porter's place in the said office.

In this manner Venality and the Cursed Spirit of Traffic pervades Everything. For a Monied Man may even buy himself into Church or State, or the Legislature. So it is no wonder they so earnestly plead for open and unlimited Traffic in our Lands, Provisions, and like great Babylon Even in Slaves and the Souls of Men.

But I contend that many things are too sacred and of too great importance to the Happiness and Dignity of the Human Race to be trafficked in, and in order to put a stop to all illicit Trade I begin with prohibiting all Commerce in Land, for that is the Root of all the other Branches of injurious Trade.

What does it signify whether the Form of a Government be Monarchial or Republican while Estates can be acquired? Will the Officers of any Government rest content to be the Guardians of other People's Estates without wishing to acquire such desirable Settlements to themselves and Posterity? Believe it not. Therefore, while Estates can be Either purchased or acquired in any manner all Governments will be rapacious and traitorous, and all men villains.

Look over to France and see what their Bonapartes, their Consuls, their Generals, and all their Public Functionaries are doing. Why, they are making Fortunes and acquiring Estates as fast as they can. And do you think small Estates will serve them? No, truly! Estates like Kingdoms were never yet large enough for their Possessors. Therefore it is absolutely necessary in order to Establish Honesty in the Earth to abolish private Property in Land.

Objection 5. — "The lower Orders now would certainly become the Drones then".

How strangely these Great People and their Advocates treat us poor devils! I wonder why we are to become Drones then more than now? Does he think the Rents will support us all in Idleness? If nobody work I am afraid there will be little Rent paid. Perhaps he thinks the higher classes will work and pay the Rents and the lower Classes will spend them. This in the simplicity of my heart I had no apprehension of seeing the great aversion they have to support idle people even though they be blind. But to be serious. He should first consider that though the people would have public Estates they would also have public charges to defray. There would be first the National Government to provide for, next the Provincial, and lastly the Parochial, before anything could be divided, so in some Parishes, perhaps, there would be no great deal coming to each one's share. For it is only what remains of the Public Money after the Public Expenses are paid that will be shared among the People to spend or live idly upon.

But where would be the great harm if some Men should but perform half their ordinary work if they be content with half wages or half gains? It would only make Employment for more Hands. And in a State where Every Person must do something or Else feel the Consequences of his Idleness there would be Enough of Work done for the happiness of Society though Men should not be always toiling like Slaves.

It is foolish to take notice of such silly Objections, but there is no End to the Stumbling blocks which these Aristocrats throw in our way. They cannot bear to see us Endeavouring to act for ourselves. They would make us believe that the more they rob us, the better we thrive! That we would rather work for any Body than ourselves, and that like Stumbling Horses we must have Riders on our backs to keep our Heads up.

How provoking it is to have to answer such villainous suggestions! But their cry and their object is the same with the old Taskmaster Pharoh. Ye are idle! Ye are idle! says he: when the People began to talk of Keeping Holiday and going into the Wilderness to worship. So instead of allowing them Holidays he increased their Tasks and ordered them to make Bricks without straw. Thus too our Taskmasters because we talk of Liberty take care to manage matters so that we should be closely employed and instead of working only six Days a Week we are obliged to work at the rate of Eight or Nine, and yet can hardly subsist. – And still the cry is work! Work! Ye are idle! Ye are idle!

To behold the Houses of Industry for the Blind and the Lame, the Old and the Young, you would think this must indeed be an industrious Nation and that there were no Drones.

But when you view Swarms of idle Quality and People of

Conditions sporting and rioting in all the Dissipation and Luxury imaginable you may then guess the Cause why all this outcry is about work, for well they know that some People must labour to uphold such a shameful mass of Extravagance and Idleness.

O Moses! what a generous plan didst thou form! Thou wast not afraid of thy lower Classes turning Drones by good usage. Thou indulgingly ordainest Holidays and Times of Rejoicing out of number. New Moons, and Sabbaths, and Jubilees, Feasts of Trumpets, Feasts of Tabernacles, etc., and liberal Sacrifices which were Feasts of hospitality and Love, where the Priest and the Stranger and the Proprietor all sat down to eat and regale together. Neither wast thou churlishly afraid of thy People tasting cheering beverage; for thou generously ordered them it at a distance from the place of worship to turn the usual offerings in Kind into Money, and take it up with them and there spend it in strong Drink, or whatsoever their soul lusted after. Even the Popes ordained Holidays in abundance and Times of Feastings, and giving Gifts and making merry; nay, their Monasteries with all their faults were often Blessings and Asylums for the Distrest both in body and mind.

But we, God help us! have fallen under the power of the hardest set of Masters that ever existed. After swallowing, up every species of common property and what belonged to religious societies and townships, they now begrudge us Every Comfort of life. Everything almost is reckoned an unbecoming luxury to such scum of the Earth, to such a Swinish multitude. They are always preaching up temperance, labour, patience and submission, and that Education only tends to render us unhappy, by refining our feelings, exhalting our ideas, and spoiling us for our low Avocations. And as to Marriage they tell us such Beggars should not multiply their kind.

But to return to the rich Man's Advocate. There is not the least reason to suppose that the system I offer would produce Idleness but rather the contrary, for there would then be no such Examples of worthless drones as we behold now in our Gentry, their Dependants and their Armies. Would not the

People then have Wives, Children, Relations, and Magistrates to spur them on to Industry? And surely there would be some vanity to gratify, and wants both natural and artificial to provide for, as well as now. And though they be exempt from all taxes and have some little help from their shares of what remains of the Public Money, yet still will they be obliged to do something towards their subsistence or else live very poorly indeed, for I do not suppose the Industrious would wish to support sturdy Beggars then more than now. The very Women and Children would cry out against what would affect them so much. But I rather think the uncommon Freedom, and Security of Property in such a happy state would operate as a stimulus rather than a Check to Industry. Though indeed there would not exist that dire necessity for incessant labour as in these deplorable Times.
London, Feb.5th, 1801.

LETTER 1

London, July 19, 1800.

Citizen,

You see I am not forgetful of your request, that I should communicate such reflections as occurred to me concerning the means of improving the happiness of mankind, but in doing this it is necessary I should allow myself a sufficient latitude in treating subjects of such importance, for how shall a man that is not free himself point out the ways of Freedom to others?

It is said in the beginning of the Bible that Man was made to till the ground and have dominion over the whole Animal Creation. All this is self evident, for he is indeed as it were the God of this lower World, and his faculties both of body and mind sufficiently qualify him for this arduous task. But here the Lordship of Man ought to stop. For as Milton and Reason say,

"Man over Man, he made not Lord."

Happy would Mankind have been had their Ambition been thus bounded by Nature. But the Earliest records show, that the Earth was immediately "filled with violence", and that

God-like reason was as much Employed in the destruction and Robbery of Fellow-Creatures, as in subduing the Earth and the Brute Creation for a more comfortable subsistance: Thus in proportion as the comforts of life increased by Man's labour and Ingenuity, so did the rapacity of men also increase to rob each other, and societies were as much formed for the sake of strengths to plunder others, as for mutual defence. Well and truly then might it be said that "the wickedness of Man was Great in the Earth", and that "all flesh had corrupted his way upon the Earth.[3]

"'Thus Societies, Families, and Tribes being originally nothing but Banditties they esteemed War and Pillage to be honourable, and the greatest Ruffians seize on the principal shares of the spoils as well of Land as Movables, introduced into the World all the curst varieties of Lordship, Vassalage, and Slavery as we see it at this Day.

"'Now Citizen, if we really want to get rid of these Evils from amongst Men, we must destroy not only personal and hereditary Lordship, but the cause of them, which is Private Property in Land. For this is the Pillar that supports the Temple of Aristocracy. Take away this Pillar, and the whole Fabric of their Dominion falls to the ground. Then shall no other Lords have dominion over us, but the Laws, and Laws too of our own making; for at present it is those who have robbed us of our lands, that have robbed us also of the privilege of making our own Laws: so in truth and reality we are in bondage, and vassalage to the landed interest. Wherefore let us bear this always in mind, and we shall never be at a loss to know where the root of the Evil lies.'"

"'Then what can be the cure but this? Namely, that the land shall no longer be suffered to be the property of individuals, but of the parishes. The rents of this Parish Estate, shall be deemed the equal property of Man, Woman, and Child, whether old or young, rich or poor, legitimate or illigitimate.'" But more of this hereafter.

I remain, yours, etc.

LETTER 2[4]

London, Aug.1st, 1800.

Citizen,

Reflecting on the number of Lives lost every summer by people bathing in improper places, and considering the easiness with which convenient and safe Bathing places may be made about most Towns and Villages, I could not help thinking the trifling expense required for such useful works, but very improperly saved. I need not direct how such Baths might be made, as there is no want of Baths for patterns; and where there are Water Works as here at London, that convey the water everywhere, the difficulty would be trifling, and a small current or pipe of water conducted to such a place would sufficiently keep it sweet and clean.

There are many places in the Country where they have small rivers and brooks so naturally forming themselves into basins sufficiently deep and spacious, that they want but little labour to render them convenient and safe Baths, where men might swim and yet Boys be in no danger. It being chiefly for the sake of safety that such places, are required they should never exceed in the deepest places four feet and a half. The good effects of such Baths would be that everybody would venture freely where they knew there was no danger, and both learn to swim and promote their health, and also great anxiety would be taken from the minds of parents and relations, for the safety of young people at such seasons. And if a wall were carried round such places both for the sake of decency and shelter from the weather, the consequence would be, that many grown people at other seasons than the hottest, would frequent them for the benefit of their health. Indeed Citizen I think such works only require to be properly recommended to be carried into execution, either by voluntary subscription, or at the expense of the parishes.

I remain, yours, etc.

LETTER 3.

London, Aug.8th, 1800.

Citizen,

As nothing attracts my attention more at present than the hue and cry raised everywhere against Monopolisers and Forestallers on account of this artificial Famine, let us see whether such a scene of villany could be transacted under such a Constitution of things as I hinted at in my first letter. You remember that I there gave the land to the parishes, by which means I broke the Monopoly of land which is the mother of all other Monopolies. Other Monopolies cannot subsist after the Fall of that, for the following reasons, viz.: First, because the Inhabitants of every Parish being the proprietors of all the soil within their respective Parishes, they will take care that the Farms shall be of such size, and let on such terms, and leases as shall appear to be most for the public good. In consequence of this, we may suppose that Farms would be so small, that the Farmers would hardly be rich enough to hoard much, neither would they be so few in numbers as easily to combine to raise the price of their produce.

Secondly, to ward against the danger that might arise to the public from the inability of these little Farmers to reserve large stocks of Corn, which might be of use in a time of scarcity, every Parish would have a public Granary, in which they would lay up every season a certain quantity of Grain in proportion to their population. This like every other public expense would be defrayed out of the rental revenue of the parish, and would only be felt by the people for the first year or two, for after that they could always sell off as much of the oldest corn as would purchase the new. Also the parishes might lay up stores of Coals, or anything else liable to accidental scarcity to prevent want, and individual Monopoly.

"'Thus Citizen you see, I have put my people in a way to destroy all Monopoly, and also effectually to provide against real famines with ease, and all by the simple operation of rendering the people what they ought to be, Lords of their own Districts.'"

You will think perhaps that people would be discouraged

from cultivation and from commerce, if the parishes interfered in this manner, and engrossed so much of the business to themselves as corporate bodies.

To this I answer that they would be wiser than to usurp the trade of the Country, for the sake of trade, but only in such matters as an experience showed the Public Safety required. Besides if such a people as this had not wisdom who had such freedom to acquire, and make use of it, where must we expect it? For consider there would be none of your great quality, nor proud landed Men, nor their minions to quash every project that does not first or last tend to increase their revenues. My people would give every one a fair hearing that had anything to propose for the public good. Neither would they long preserve in wrong measures, if they should chance to fall into them, because no obstacle remained to hinder them to change them.

In the advanced state of learning which the World is now arrived at, there can be no want of cultivated abilities everywhere sufficient to conduct the Public Business. All that is wanting is, a good system in which Men being placed in a state of equality and freedom, the reasoning faculties would be encouraged to expand to the utmost. And such a system Citizen is this, which I have given you a sketch of.

I remain, yours, etc.

LETTER 4

London, Aug.18th, 1800.

Citizen,

The late attempt of some of our Legislature to amend the Laws relating to adultery, could not but attract your attention as well as mine. But I think better preventatives have been adopted by a neighbouring Nation, than any proposed in our Parliament.

The facility of Divorce which the French now allow, must have the happiest effects. The matrimonial couples need not always now be chiding each other to no purpose about misconduct, for as they know they can part so easily they must if they wish to continue together study to make each other happy by sobriety, industry, civility, etc. Gross faults will not always be borne with now by either side therefore disgraceful bickerings will cease and the nuptial state will become like a continual Courtship, because a good Husband or good Wife will be valued, and used as they deserve through fear of being lost.

Another good effect must also flow from such known possibility of separation. Men will no longer be afraid to give a beloved Woman a fair trial of domestic Life, though formerly she may have borne but a loose character, by which many will be reclaimed, the number of Single Women lessened, and the state of Society much mended.

But under our unalterable Establishment what a dreadful thing it is to make a wrong choice where there is no Remedy nor Redress for life. It is enough to make one shudder to think of being indissolubly bound to a Spendthrift, a Drunkard, a Sluggard, a Tyrant, a Brute, a Trollop, a Vixen. — What signifies Reforms of Government or Redress of Public Grievances, if people cannot have their domestic grievances redressed? If they must behold Ruin and Disgrace overwhelming them like a Deluge without any Power of Prevention?

This Subject is so feelingly understood in this country, that it is supposed the Chains of Hymen would be among the first that would be broken, in case of a Revolution, and the family business of life turned over to Cupid, who though he may be a little whimsical, is not so stern an jailor like a Deity.

I remain, yours, etc.

LETTER 5
London, Sept.20th, 1800.

Citizen,

The unprecedented clearness of provisions, sets every head on devising how to find a Remedy. And as people impute much of the mischief to the manner Gentlemen now follow of letting their Lands in large Farms, they talk of having Laws made to reduce Farms again to a moderate size. But this is reckoning without their Host. This is like the mice tying a Bell about the Cat's neck. Whose to do it? Are not our Legislators all Landlords? And are they going to make Laws to restrict themselves in the management of their property? Believe it not. They find those rich Tenants both give them more Rent, and pay more certainly than poor Men could. Neither bad seasons, nor accidents among Cattle, affect them. They are still able in spite of every mischance to pay, and also to hoard and keep up what they have, till they can get a price to their mind. All this the Landlord knows is for his advantage and makes him look on the increasing profits of the Farmer with pleasure, as he will be sure to advance his Rent in proportion at the expiration of his Lease. These Landed Legislators therefore rejoice when Markets are high, and will open and shut the Ports, and give Bounties out of the national purse for the exportation of grain, rather than the Farmers shall be hurt.

"'It is childish therefore to expect ever to see Small Farms again, or ever to see anything else than the utmost screwing and grinding of the poor, till you quite overturn the present system of Landed Property. For they have got more completely into the spirit and power of oppression now than ever was known before, and they hold the people in defiance by means of their armed associations. They are now like a warlike enemy quartered upon us for the purpose of raising contributions, and William the Conqueror and his Normans were fools to them in the Art of fleecing. Therefore anything short of total Destruction of the power of these Samsons will not do. And that must be accomplished, not by simple shaving which leaves the roots of their strength to grow again. No: we must scalp them or else they will soon recover and pull our Temple of Liberty about our Ears.[5]

We must not leave even their stump in the Earth, like Nebuchadnezzar though guarded by a band of Iron. For ill destroyed Royalty and Aristocracy, will be sure to recover and overspread the Earth again as before. And when they are suffered to return again to their former Dominion it is always with ten-fold more rage and policy, and so the condition of their wretched subjects is quickly rendered worse as a reward for their too tender resistance.[6]

In plain English nothing less than complete Extermination of the present system of holding Land in the manner I propose will ever bring the World again to a state worth living in.

"'But how is this mighty work to be done? I answer it must be done at once. For it will be sooner done at once than at twice or at an hundred times. For the public mind being suitably prepared by reading my little Tracts and conversing on the subject, a few Contingent Parishes have only to declare the land to be theirs and form a convention of Parochial Delegates. Other adjacent Parishes would immediately on being invited follow the example, and send also their Delegates and thus would a beautiful and powerful New Republic instantaneously arise in full vigour. The power and resources of War passing in this manner in a moment, into the hands of the People from the hands of their Tyrants, they, like sham Samsons would become weak and harmless as other Men. And being thus as it were scalped of their Revenues and the Lands that produced them their Power would never more grow to enable them to overturn our Temple of Liberty.

"'Therefore talk no more of impossibilities. How lately have we seen Unions of the People sufficiently grand and well conducted to give sure hopes of success? Abroad and at Home, in America, France, and in our own Fleets, we have seen enough of public spirit, and extensive unanimity in the present generation to accomplish Schemes of infinitely greater difficulty than a thing that may be done in a Day, when once the public mind is duly prepared. In fact it is like the Almighty saying 'Let there be light and it was so'. So the People have only to say 'Let the Land be ours', and it will be so.

"'For who, pray, are to hinder the People of any Nation from doing so when they are inclined? Are the Landlords in the Parishes more numerous and powerful in proportion to the People than the brave warlike Officers in our own mutinous Fleets were to their Crews?[7]

Certainly not. Then Landsmen have nothing to fear more than Seamen, and indeed much less for after such a Mutiny on Land, the Masters of the People would never become their Masters again, whereas, the poor Sailors had to submit again to their former Masters, as they well know to their cost. And as they accomplished their Mutinies without bloodshed, so may Landsmen be assured if unanimous of accomplishing their Deliverance in the same harmless manner.[8]

But some that hanker after the Flesh-pots of Egypt, and all the luxuries accompanying Oppression, would not have the Landed Interest quite rooted out but only melt down by degrees the large Estates into little ones, and a deal of pretty stuff like this.

Do not these drivellers consider, that little seeds produce great Trees? That little principalities are the seeds of great Empires? And that these little Freeholders would frequently be buying and selling and marrying among themselves till they brought us back to the same inequality in which we are? Did not the Jews, the Spartans, the Romans, and the Saxons give us sufficient specimens of the instability of this little Freehold System? Where are they now? Are they not all overwhelmed and swallowed up, while nothing but systems of Monopoly remain?

But those Nations though they went great lengths in their Agrarian Laws could never establish complete equality in Estates. For great numbers were obliged to go without any land and were even in a state of Slavery, and bought and sold like Cattle. Surely we do not want such ignoble doings again in the Earth? We are better off as we are. For pride accompanies Land to such a degree that the Smallest Freeholder is possessed with all the aristocratic haughtiness and contempt for his fellow creatures as the greatest Duke, and is much more insufferable on account of his greater ignorance. So the fewer we have of such detestable overbearing Breed, the better, and we then can the sooner destroy them, when we please.

Therefore away with the whole Root of the Evil! Let us no longer foolishly think of dividing the Land, but only the Rents; which is a thing practical and easy, whether we increase in number or diminish.

I remain, yours, etc.

POSTSCRIPT

In order to show how far we are cut off from the rights of Nature, and reduced to a more contemptible stage than the

Brutes, I will relate an affair I had with a Forester in a Wood near Hexham alone by myself a gathering of Nuts, the Forester popped through the Bushes upon me, and asking what I did there, I answered gathering Nuts: Gathering Nuts! said he, and dare you say so? Yes, said I, why not? Would you question a Monkey, or a Squirrel, about such a Business? And am I to be treated as inferior to one of those Creatures? Or have I a less right? But who are you, continued I, that thus take upon you to interrupt me? I'll let you know that, said he when I lay you fast for trespassing here. Indeed! answered I. But how can I trespass here where no Man ever planted or cultivated, for these Nuts are the spontaneous Gifts of Nature ordained alike for the Sustenance of Man and Beast, that choose to gather them, and therefore they are common. I tell you, said he, this Wood is no Common. It belongs to the Duke of Portland. Oh! My service to the Duke of Portland, said I, Nature knows no more of him than of me. Therefore, as in Nature's storehouse the Rule is, "First come, first served", so the Duke of Portland must look sharp if he wants any Nuts. But in the name of Seriousness, continued I, must not one's privileges be very great in a country where we dare not pluck a Hazel Nut? Is this an Englishman's Birthright? Is it for this we are called upon to serve in the Militia, to defend this Wood and this Country, against the Enemy.[9]

"'What must I say to the French, if they come? If they jeeringly ask me what I am fighting for? Must I tell them for my Country? For my dear Country in which I dare not pluck a Nut? Would not they laugh at me? Yes. And do you think I would bear it? No: Certainly I would not. I would throw down my Musket saying let such as the Duke of Portland, who claim the Country, fight for it, for I am but a stranger and sojourner, and have neither Part nor Lot amongst them.[10]

This reasoning had such an effect on the Forester that he told me to gather as many Nuts as I pleased.

LETTER 6
London, Sept.25th, 1800.

Citizen,

The other Day one of the Labourers belonging to the East

India Warehouses being in my company, and knowing he could confide in me, opened his Mind pretty freely concerning the present riots, and told me that several of their people had been discharged for saying they would bite off the Bullets from their Cartridges if they were ordered to fire at the mob, for, continues he, we in general wish the People well, and their Cause, and would be sorry to hurt them; but I don't like their breaking the Lamps and Windows. Besides, adds he, they are too audacious and provoking, I, myself, was struck on the head with a stone.

You should keep better company, said I. How can they pry into your heart to know whether you mean them well or not? But they are at no loss to know that your appearance against them with Arms in your Hands is to keep them in awe, and encourage the Monopolisers, and all their oppressors. Therefore if you would be thought to mean well to the people, and the Redress of Grievances, lay down your Arms, for that is the best way to manifest to both Parties, that you will not abet nor countenance such Rapacity. But if you value your place more than your conscience, or Humanity, think it but right to be knocked on the head.

It is thus, Citizen, that needy, mercenary and interested Men, though of more than vulgar knowledge assist in riveting the Chains of their Fellow-creatures instead of contributing to break them. Fie upon it! that Man should show more Courage and Steadiness in defending the cause of their Masters, though ever so bad, than the cause of their Fellows and Equals, though ever so just, till at length they are depressed to a state below humanity.

I have often thought how much superior the Condition of Reptiles is to that of human nature, in the present perverted state of things.

A Worm pays no Rent: the Earth while he lives is his portion, and he riots in untaxed Luxuries. And, if perchance, a Crow, or other creature, should pick him up, why that is only Death, which must come in some shape or other to us all as well as he. But in this respect he had the advantage of us that while he lived he paid no Rent! And herein are all the Creatures to be envied.

Thus, though one Species preys on another, there is no Bondage, no Slavery, in the Case; it is only plain Death, Could our oppressors free us from Death, that would be something gained, in lieu of our Liberty. But ours, God help us! is entirely a losing game. Instead of saving us from Destruction, they accelerate our Death a thousand ways. For, by their villianous Wars, and artificial Famines, they dig Millions of untimely Graves.

Blame me not then Citizen, for so earnestly pressing a political evils, and render the State of Man as happy as it ought to be.

I remain, yours, etc.

LETTER 7

London, Oct.8th, 1800.

Citizen,

Monopoly is injustice, let it be of what kind it will, whether of Government, Land, or Trade, therefore I cannot help abhoring that National thirst of ours, after the universal Trade of the World, to the prejudice of all other Nations.

But this external Monopoly, is plainly the offspring of our internal Monopoly. For the same Covetousness which is nourished at Home, by the oppression of Fellow-citizens expands like ambition in its Maturity till it grasps at the whole Earth. Neither would the Moon or Planets elude our harpy claws, could we but find a passage thither, and we should soon hear of companies established to monopolise the Celestial trade also.

Ought not therefore, such avaricious Madness to be pitied, and like other Madness curbed by Force? I think it possible. And, if so, for the peace of the World it certainly should be accomplished. But, be not surprised, Citizen, when you see me again recur to my old specific. For I am fully convinced that my simple plan of destroying the impious Monopoly of Land, is the grand Panacea that will cure all manner of evils arising from Avarice and Ambition.

Consider, Citizen, whether a Nation which had no public stocks to traffic in, and whose Land, as I propose, should all belong to the parishes, would hunger and thirst after the

Riches of the World, to the pernicious degree that is now common. For observe, though they should acquire the Riches of Peru, they could only speculate in fair and honest Trade, and Manufactures. For, as I said, the Parishes being so well able, out of their Rents, to supply every exigence of the Government upon the spur of the occasion, there could not possibly be any National Debt or Funds. Neither could they root, or concentrate their acquirements in Land to give their Names to, as the Psalmist says, and invest them in their worthless heirs. So that Men would learn to moderate their desires, and cease to aspire after boundless wealth, which they could have no means of consolidating.

Neither could such a Nation be fond of Conquest for the same Reason, because if they wished for the continuance of their own Constitution at Home (which I believe they would not willingly part with) they must be careful how they introduce a sudden inundation of wealth from abroad. So, if they were forced by an Implacable Enemy to conquer him, they would be systematically compelled to establish in that Country their own Constitution, as the best Means of rendering it in future a pacific and good Neighbour.

It would be highly dangerous, to their System of Liberty and Equality, to have their Citizens pompously established abroad like Princes, under the Denomination of Prefects or Governors, and swelling into unmanigable power on the spoils of foreign Provinces. The Histories of all Republics will woefully teach them to beware of such destructive Rocks.

But, you will perhaps say, the Revenues arising from foreign Conquests and Provinces, appear very alluring and flattering to any People, and, if brought home to the national Treasury, might in proportion to their quantity, lessen the Land-taxes of the Parishes. But this would be a deceitful and dangerous easement. For a Government that draws great Riches from sources which do not immediately affect the people, as from Loans, Mines, Foreign Tribute or Subsidies, is sure to creep by Degrees into absolute power and overturn everything.

It is for this reason I would not have the Land national, nor provincial, but parochial property, that the People might be as much interested as possible, both in the improvement of their estates, which thus would be always under their eye, and in the expenditure of all public monies, which would be paid straight out of their Revenues, even while in their hands, and when just going into their pockets. The Government being supplied in this hard but honest way, by the General, Land-taxes sent regularly, would neither be suffered, nor require, to have a rich Treasury. Therefore a Government so supported, without Revenue Officers, and very few Placemen at home, and none abroad, could not be very dangerous to Liberty.

You may be apt to think this Discouragement to the Monopoly of Foreign Trade and Conquest, will tend to bring on a National apathy and disgust to Labour and Business, and that stimulating motives will be wanting to prevent the return of Barbarism.

No such thing, Citizen, such a people will have incentives enough to Industry and to improve rather than decline in Civilisation.

In the first place they will be all well educated, having schools, and perhaps Libraries, at the expense of the parishes. Reading promotes refinement and sensibility, and a Taste for Elegance in Clothes, Furniture and Every Department in Life. Now, it is only Labour, Industry, and Ingenuity that can administer Gratification to this multiplication of refined Desires; therefore Trade, Manufactures, and the Arts must needs be greatly encouraged. And as all Nations, however barbarous or civilised, have naturally a taste for foreign Productions and Luxuries, and will do anything they can to acquire them, so may we expect this People.

A working and ingenious people can never want wherewith to barter for the produce of other climes, and, if so, will have Trade enough without having recourse to the expedient of great, avaricious, monopolising Companies like us, who for their private ends, disturb the Peace of the whole World, setting Nation against Nation, and People against People, till the whole Earth and Sea is turned into an Aceldama.

Surely nothing can be wanting to encourage both Trade and Labour, but open Ports, Liberty and Security of Property.

For where is the People so barbarous that will not trade, and be stimulated by it to labour, hunt, fish, and exert their abilities to the utmost, for Articles to traffic with, unless interrupted by some malignant, tyrannical power? So, as nothing can be got without Labour, there can be no reason to fear that a people so enlightened, and enjoying such unparalleled security, under Laws of their own making can ever degenerate into sloth, and all its disgustful consequences.

Wherefore to conclude. As Mediocrity of Wealth has always been found to be the never failing source of Knowledge, Good Taste, Industry and Happiness, and of all the virtues, I can harbour no apprehensions for the welfare of my Commonwealth.

I remain, yours, etc.

LETTER 8

London, Oct.9th, 1800.

Citizen,

I have often amused myself with comparing the superior degrees of Happiness which I supposed people of such Callings and Stations in Life would enjoy in my Commonwealth, above what they now enjoy under the present system of things, and shall at this time take a glance at the Mariners.

In the first place, as my Commonwealth can have no interest in War, as made appear in my last, so the sailors can have no Press-gangs to fear.

And in the next place, as the Government is entirely supported by one simple Tax which is the Land-tax, and therefore has no occasion to raise the Revenue on Trade, either on Exportation, or Importation, the Mariner will be free from the plague of Custom House Officers.

He being thus at full Liberty to fetch and carry like a man on Land, from one village or town to another, it may naturally be expected that every Man and Boy on board of a Vessel, will turn Merchant and condition with their Master for a certain portion of Stowage Room for their goods. Sailors having such Liberty and Privileges, would soon become quite another set of people than what they are at present. Instead of the desperate, careless, reprobate character, which the

Commonmen now generally acquire, they would become provident and sober, and solicitous to provide for their Families and their own subsistence in old age.

In consequence of such improvement and the desirable Commodities conveyed by them from Clime to Clime, they would always be welcomed and respected wherever they came, as a most valuable Class of Men. In short Citizen, their improved Condition would be beyond all description. For as all the children of the Commonwealth would partake of the good education of the Country before they were suffered to go to Business of any kind so would those who went to Sea.

Then let us push forward to that joyful Day, when all shall be happy by Land and by Sea.

I remain, yours, etc.

LETTER 9
London, Oct.12th, 1800.

Citizen,

After providing so well for the Seamen, you will naturally expect I should appease the apprehensions of Four Classes of Men, who will be thrown out of employ by the adoption of my Constitution. Those four Classes are:

First, Landlords and Stockholders who subsist on Revenues extorted legally as they say, from the Rest of Mankind and are called Quality and Gentry.

Secondly, Lawyers, Attorneys, etc., who subsist almost entirely by conveying Landed Property from one to another, and in Litigations about it.

Thirdly, Gentlemen's Servants of every description.

Lastly, Soldiers and Sailors employed in War.

Now Citizen it becomes us to pay particular attention to the first Class, for they have always been the principal care of every author especially of the great Mr Burke, of aristocratic memory.

Well then, at the creation of the Commonwealth when the mighty Fiat of the People has gone forth and at the sound of the Landlords of the Earth, and the Creditors of the State, are annihilated the Condition of the ci-devant Quality will stand thus.

In the first place they will find the People in their great lenity and generosity to have spared their Lives, and also their Money, Plate, Jewels, Furniture, Apparel, Cattle and movable Effects of Every Kind. And in the next place as an equivalent for their lost Land, and Money in the Stocks, they will find themselves in the full possession of the rights of citizenship, in the fostering bosom of the most human and just Commonwealth that ever existed.[11]

Now Citizen I wish to know, after landing these people so safely on the other side of this dreaded Revolution, and withal so richly provided, they ought still to be pitied? Or whether some might not think they had been suffered to escape with too much of the spoils which they and their Forefathers had squeezed from poor suffering Humanity? Might not these People being still the richest Class, though they had lost their Lands and Money in the Funds, be well content to be quiet, less by stirring they should compel the people in their own defence to exterminate them, and sequester also the Remainder of their ill gotten Wealth. Yes, verily, I think they may be glad and rest well satisfied with their happy lot.

Query. But will not they lead a melancholy life, reflecting on the goodly Estates and Pensions, which they have lost and all their other ample Revenues? And, how must they subsist without an Income for their movable Effects though ever so considerable, will dwindle away?

What! Are these pampered people, these Monopolisers of the Earth, these Stockholders, these Placemen and Pensioners, this tyrannical Crew under which we groan; to furnish Rents and Taxes, for whom we starve ourselves and families, and suffer the privation of every comfort that renders Life desirable: I say are these Locusts to be eternally held up to us as objects of Charity and Commisseration, though we so generously suffer them still to remain the Richest members of the Community, and adopt those people for Fellow-citizens, that reject us, nay that treat us as of a different species? For shame! Urge not another word in favour of such undeserving objects.

And suppose now these high-minded Beggars should still

wish to continue in their former Extravagance and Luxury, till the whole of the Effects which the good natured People shall leave them be spent: Are we for ever bound to uphold them in such doings?

But on the other Hand, if they rather wish prudently to submit to their fate, most of them will find that they have Effects sufficient, with a small share of economy, to maintain themselves luxuriously, without Work or Industry all their Lives, especially in a Nation where everything will be cheap, and free of Taxes. And if they further submit to turn their Talents and Property to Trade, their superior Capital cannot fail of yielding a genteel and happy Livelihood. Let therefore all this Superfluity of Concern for any Class, but especially for the richest cease, and let this incomparable Jubilee, this New Creation be celebrated with that universal Joy and Fraternity becoming so grand an occasion.

Query. But as there can be no Law to compel people to Economy and Industry, what will be the fate of these idle-bred people, if they should prodigally spend all, and reduce themselves to Beggary? D——n these idle-bred People, I was going to say. But I'll try to keep my temper. This query seems entirely superfluous. For I have said all along that after all public expenses are paid out of the Rents, the remainder will be equally divided among all the Men, Women, and Children in the Parish whether Poor or Rich. Because neither Riches nor Poverty can disqualify a person from a participation of Natural Rights. So then even though we should suppose our quondam Betters will so far disgrace themselves as to act like thoughtless Profligates and reduce themselves to the lowest ebb of Poverty, yet will they have as well as others, their said Shares of the Public Money that is returned to the People. But if notwithstanding all these Helps and favourable Situations, some high-bred Personages should think it more for their Honour bravely to rush into the danger of starvation, there will yet be another Resource in the Humanity and Wisdom of the Country, and such Lunatics no doubt, would be suitably taken care of. Though I do not suppose they would degrade their Fellow-Creatures, as is done at present, by cramming them into the Poor-houses among the most degenerate of the Species in their Distress, but would rather grant them small Pensions which, in addition to their Rental Dividends, would comfortably maintain them at the Fire-side of their Friends.

Now Citizen, having got these troublesome Gentry off my hand I shall find but small difficulty in disposing of the other three Classes because they are neither so high-bred nor so little used to Industry, and therefore can the more easily accommodate themselves to some useful calling by Sea or Land suitable to their Genius and Circumstances. And even at the worst, if some of them should turn out as worthless as we supposed the Quality, they would also find the same Resources in the parishes.

It is impossible but there should be some partial Losses and Inconveniences attending so radical a Revolution, but when the sufferers reflected how much the State of Society was improved, they could not say they had no equivalent.

I remain, yours, etc.

LETTER 10

London, Oct.14th, 1800.

Citizen,

It is said in the first Chapter of the Acts of the Apostles, that Judas purchased a Field with the Reward of Iniquity, and that it was called the Field of Blood.

Now Citizen if we go to Examine but very superficially into the manner that most Fields and Estates have been acquired either formerly or now-a-days, I am afraid too much blood and iniquity will appear in the business.

There are but two Ways of inheriting the Earth agreeable to Justice and the Rights of Man: The first is in the Patriarchal and Indian manner by using it as a common Grazing Pasture and Hunting Park, as was done by Abraham, Isaac, and Jacob, and Esau and Ishmael. The second is by letting out in Farms and Tenements for Cultivation and Habitation as at present, but reserving the Rents to the People of the District in lieu of their Rights of Pasturage, and Hunting.

The first Mode was naturally fallen into by the rudest of Mankind, as it were by Instinct, but we could hardly expect the adoption of the Second, till Experience showed the Evils they must Endure, on departing from the Simplicity of the first, and introducing private Property in Land.

It was owing to the Villainies practised in the way of getting private possessions, the Wars necessary for their Defence from other Intruders, and the Enslaving of Men for the cultivation of them that the Rechabites were enjoined by their Father, neither to build Houses, Sow Seed, Plant Vineyard nor have any but to live in Tents; and thus by beginning anew the Pastoral and Patriarchal Mode of Life exhibit to the jarring World an example of primeval Innocence.

Now we find the Rechabites were far from being despised, for adopting and following those simple old-fashioned customs, but on the contrary we see the Usurper Jehu, honourably saluting Jonadab, the son of Rechab, and taking him into his Chariot to be a witness of the Vengeance he was executing on the encroaching monopolising House of Ahab. We find likewise Jeremiah the prophet making honourable mention of this Family of the Rechabites for adhering so closely to the innocent pastoral Institutions enjoined by their Father.

If these just Men had conceived the possibility of preserving the just Rights of Man in a State of Cultivation by dividing the Rents, they would certainly have adopted such a Mode, rather than forego the conveniences attending such a condition, but as they did not they were excusable in going back again to their original state rather than be concerned in the villainous Transactions attending Private Possession.

Now Citizen, a practical way of reconciling the Rights of Man, with a State of Cultivation having as you see been plainly proposed, the World can no longer live with Innocence, or the least plausible excuse in the present monopolising unjust state.

If the Rechabites were so struck with abhorrence at the proceeding of Ahab and Jezebel in the disinheritance and murder of Naboth, that they retired from the comforts and pleasures of Towns and Cultivation, what feelings must we have, who with all the Villainies of History, as well as the Enormities of our Contemporaries, and Neighbours before our Eyes in this diabolical business of acquiring possessions, can wish to continue a day longer in a state so repugnant to every human feeling.[12]

Do we still wish to see such Men as Judas as General Monk, as Villainous Ministers, as Jailors, and Bastille Keepers, as citizen killing Generals and Admirals, as our Monopolisers of every description, with all the Tribes of Nabobs and Slave Traders from the East and West Indies, each coming with the Reward of Iniquity in his Hand to buy a Field of Blood.

Can we expect to enjoy Liberty and the Rights of Man, in the midst of such Neighbours, who founded their Estates in Blood and must continue them in oppression? In endless, and increasing oppression? For they still cry, more! more! another vineyard! I have not yet enough! My Family is not yet sufficiently aggrandised.

Thus you see Citizen, that all the Traitors and Robbers of Mankind wish like Judas to bury and secure their spoils in the Earth in Fields of Blood. Let us therefore prevent it, by taking the Earth into our own hands, and convert it from being the means of our greatest evils, to our greatest good.

I remain, yours, etc.

LETTER 11
London, Oct.16th, 1800.

Citizen,

You see I do not in the old fashioned manner attempt to preach and pray the World into Justice and Tenderheartedness. No truly. I have seen enough of that kind of delusion. If Religion would have any influence on Men's Lives, we ought to be the most righteous and compassionate people on Earth. Where is there a people that abound more in preaching Men, and preaching Books, in all the Sects and persuasions, and also in Books of Morality, Satire, etc., and yet you see there is no living on account of every Species of Oppression and Monopoly. Therefore it is evident that it is only by good Laws and Constitutions that we must hope to amend our deplorable State, and not by our addressing ourselves to the Religion, Generosity, and Feelings of the Rich and Powerful, for their humiliating Charity. And it is natural and universal

Interest alone can cement our Society when established and secure us from revolving back again to our former wretchedness.

Permit me then Citizen, to return to my old Subject and show the good effects that would instantaneously be felt through the whole Nation on the adoption of my proposed Constitution.

No sooner would it be proclaimed, but the prices of every Article would begin to fall. For the Taxes and the Paper Money, which now enhance the price of everything, ceasing all at once, the difference in value, would be found very great, and the Dealers would immediately enter into a competition with each other striving who should first lower their Articles till everything found the lowest level.

The Farmers likewise would not be the last to show a disposition to supply the Markets at a reasonable Rate. For they must thenceforth look on the People as their Landlords, who either might renew their Leases or not, as they considered them well-wishers to the Public Good.

Again, in order to make comfortable Livings for poor Husbandmen the Parishes no doubt would divide the over large Farms, as soon as their Leases expired, and also be at some expense in enclosing and improving their waste ground, whether consisting of high Land, or Marshes, and suffer no space to remain in a useless and unprofitable state. For as every Person would have a most intimate feeling in the improvement of their Parish Estate, so every Parish would in fact, instantaneously and naturally become a Board of Agriculture. The consequence of which would be an immediate increase of Husbandmen, and a wholesome decrease of Artificers and Tradesmen, who are now out of all proportion too numerous.[13]

Nay I suppose many Country Parishes would find it for their advantage to invite Poor Men from the Towns, to come and settle on their waste Lands, and by advancing them a little money at first, either by way of Gift or Loan, enable to purchase some stock and utensils by which both the Community at large, would be benefitted by an increase of Provisions, and the Parish Revenues, greatly increased by the addition of the new Rents. Thus Trade and Manufactures being thinned, the more Business and Employment would be left for the remainder of the Workmen, and good Wages, would be the result in every calling, to which when added the cheapness of Provisions, and the Joys of Freedom, the happiness of Mankind would be complete.

For in Nations that did not adopt the same Constitution would be ruined. For they could not support a Competition in Trade against such a People who had no Drones in their Society. The present idle Classes being all compelled by necessity to become industrious bees in one line or other, the real Wealth of the Nation, which is the Produce of Labour would so increase, that it must in spite of every obstruction overflow, and influence all the Nations of the Earth.

I am, yours, etc.

LETTER 12

London, Oct.18th, 1800.

Citizen,

I am pleased to find that you coinside in my political opinions and plans. You also tell me you have perused my Constitution of a Perfect Commonwealth, and my other little pamphlets on the same subject, and approve of the whole. This is some satisfaction and encouragement, and I rejoice not as a vain author, but as a well-wisher to Mankind, because if these writings be capable of convincing and animating one Man of sense, they may by Parity of Reasoning be supposed in due time to convince Millions.

It is natural enough of you to wonder why none of the modern Champions of the Rights of Man should take notice of my Scheme in their Books and Harangues though I have been diligently publishing it these Six and Twenty Years, in great variety of shapes, and have sold many thousands of Copies.

But Citizen though they could not be ignorant (for I did not poor as I have been conceal my Ideas under a Bushel) yet your surprise will cease when I reflect on the purity of the plan, and the selfishness and avarice of the human heart. Can any think you, but real lovers of Justice and Equality, admire a Constitution framed according to the Exactions of Nature? — That suffers no national or confiscated Estates, or Domains to be dealt out in portions among the Orators, Writers, and Generals who may Contribute to the Establishment? — That makes no Partial distinctions of its children into happy elect and rejected Reprobates? — That omits the very Babies and their Mothers, the blind and the lame, the dumb and the eloquent to an equal participation of the Rights of Nature? I say will such a levelling Constitution as this, do for proud Men of Abilities and Conceited Excellence? No: surely. Our Reformers would have showed themselves Israelites indeed, in whom there was no guile had they heartily patronised, and pressed on Mankind so disinterested a Scheme.[14]

Then you may say why trouble myself further about such a crooked Race? Let them still go on their old way, changing names without the substance; and setting up one set of Lords, and Monopolies on the ruins of another as they have done from the beginning.

Indeed Citizen with grief I behold the indirect and suspicious modes which the professed Reformers of the World take to deliver it from oppression. For instead of striking at the Root, they only aim at the Branches. So that like some prolific vegetables the more it is hacked and hewed, the more it spreads. For the very chips and cuttings take root, and become distinct plants. But yet I hope, that when the cup of villainy is full, and Men are fairly tired out, and have lost conceit of their inconsistent Democracies and other Forms of Government: When they perceive that Mamelukes and Citizens, make but an incoherent mass, and that Men, who under the specious name of Citizens, have the Estates and Power of Lords and Princes and use them as much to the injury of Mankind; when they are fairly sick of the Wars, the Artificial Famines, and all the other Evils, springing from this bitter Root of Landed Monopoly, that then they may turn their eyes to my just Constitution, as the last, and only Remedy against all Political Evils.

You are likewise surprised that I have been suffered in these persecuting times, to print and publish a plan, that more certainly aims at the overthrow of all Establishments, than any that were ever proposed by others.

But Citizen, I do not particularly aim at the overthrow of the Government of this country, by publishing my plan. No such thing. For it is as well calculated for any nation under the Heavens, though I write it in England for the best of Reasons, viz., because, I am here and cannot help it. In consequence of this I cannot altogether avoid appearing sensible to some affairs transacting around me by which I am very intimately affected, but nevertheless, I am as abstract as possible, and ought to be considered as only advancing a Theory, which I believe would greatly increase the happiness of the World, or any part of it, that choose to give it a trial. But whether England be the first or last Country to adopt it, or whether it be adopted anywhere at all, does not rest with me. I am but an Individual, and it is now out of my power even to recall it again, and therefore must remain, whether I will or no, a mere Bystander, while it must stand or fall according to its own merit.

I remain, yours, etc.

LETTER 13
London, Oct.24th, 1800.

Citizen,

The Management of Hospitals for the Sick being of the greatest importance to the Public, nobody can be blamed for endeavouring to improve their State. And though they are of very great Public Unity, as at present conducted, yet I think they may be of much greater, by allowing an unbounded latitude and Ease of Admittance.

Is it not wonderful that Subscribers or Governors, as they call themselves to such Institutions, should so far stand on punctilios, as to require application from the poor weak patients for Letters of Recommendation, before they can be admitted.

The difficulties attending the procurement of these recommendatory papers, and the time and strength wasted about them, are often of the most hurtful tendency to poor creatures labouring under the accumulated burdens of disease and poverty and are certainly the cause of many a death. The grievances and anxieties suffered on such occasions are incomprehensible to such as have not tasted of the bitter cup. As to out-patients, their usage is shameful to an extreme, by the uncertain time of Medical Gentlemen's attendance, and makes it more to a patient's advantage if his time be of any value at all, to pay for his Medicines Elsewhere, than to fret so many hours away in waiting.

Why then in the name of Humanity, should all these disagreeable repugnances be thrown in people's way? It is doubtless to deter as many as possible from applying to such places for Relief, and induce them to apply to the faculty Elsewhere, rather than dance such distressing attendance.

So much then for the Medical Gentlemen working together for the benefit of their craft. They should therefore be looked strictly after and made to attend more punctual to their appointed time, at all such places of medical relief, for surely the time of one individual cannot be more precious than that of the many unhappy, and useful sick, who are waiting for them.

But what is the strangest of all in this melancholy business, is, that the very subscribers should wish to come in for a share of this pitiable attendance, and at the most critical time too. Good God! Can it be to squeeze a little homage from such suffering Creatures, or is it to take such a sure opportunity as this to mortify, and let them know their dependent condition? They will not dare to avow such mean motives.

Well then Citizen to remedy all these evils I would have the Hospitals open for the admission of the sick of every description, every Day of the week, without previous application. For as in cases of sickness there can be the least chance of Imposture, we may safely trust the detection of cheats to the sagacity of the Faculty who should admit all applicants immediately without making them wait for a particular Day of the Week as for the moving of the Waters. I say, let all immediately be admitted either as In or Out-patients, as the cases should require. No questions should be asked about Circumstances or Security for Funerals, neither should Maladies of any description be rejected, but only for want of Room in which case, if the Patient required to be taken in, he should be told to apply to such other Hospital as they knew to have vacancies, that no Time might be lost.

By such speedy Relief and encouraging Invitation the most happy effects would accrue to the public. Every disease would be taken in such due time, as to render the Cure almost certain, and those of an infectious nature would likewise be prevented from spreading.

Now I am speaking of infectious Diseases, let me propose the Treatment of a certain one in some such manner as the plague, which does perhaps infinitely more mischief to the Human species. Every one infected with that foul Malady, should be by Law compelled to fly to an Hospital for relief as soon as they perceived themselves injured. And to prevent either Male or Female, Old or Young, Rich or Poor from concealing their Case through Modesty large Rewards should be ordained for the discovery of such infected people, of what condition so-ever, who should immediately when discovered, be thrust into an Hospital, and there locked up in the Foul Ward till completely Cured. A penalty should also be laid on such persons as did not immediately apply to an Hospital as soon as they knew themselves infected.

This would be an effectual way to root that destructive disease out of any Country, and we should soon, yes very soon, here little or nothing of it, if so treated. Perhaps the same method taken with the Small pox, might eradicate it also. And so of every infectious disorder.

But now Citizen, methinks I hear you say, what will become of such of the Faculty as have not places in the Hospitals, for they would be ruined if such free and easy access were permitted to such Institutions.

I answer that I was not studying for the Interest of any particular set of Men, but for the public good. But supposing there were Hospitals sufficient for all the people when sick, and that there were no other Medical men employed than were placed in them, I cannot apprehend that the state of Mankind would be worse. And suppose further that Hospitals were all supported by County Rates, instead of private subscriptions that we might get rid of paying such distressing homage to Subscribers and Governors, it would certainly be a great improvement.

This business of Hospitals like all other public business, would be best conducted in my Commonwealth. For in that incomparable state everything of an extensive nature and influence beyond the bounds of a Parish, as Hospitals, Colleges, Bridges, Harbours, Roads, etc., would be supported by Provincial or County Rates of so much per pound, and the Rents of the Parishes. So that after a Parish Rents were collected, the Account of Expenditure would stand thus.

	£	s.	d.
The Total of the Rents of this Parish, collected at Midsummer Quarter in — Year of the Commonwealth	00000	0	0
Expenditure			
Paid to the State, at os. od. per £	000	0	0
Paid to the Country at os. od. per Do.	000	0	0
Expended in Parish Affairs	000	0	0
Total Expenses	00000	0	0
Paid the Remainder being ooooo o o to oooo Men, Women and Children, having Settlement in the Parish at the rate of £o. os. od. each.			

Thus one single and simple collection of the Rents serves for every Public Purpose, without the Expense and Grievances of Revenue-Officers, and Revenue Laws, and without further Toll Tax or Custom.

I remain, yours, etc.

LETTER 14

London, Dec.27, 1800.

Citizen,

When I contemplate the meagre and beggarly appearance of the working people at this deplorable period, and at the same time hear their deep and desperate exclamations, sighed forth from their broken hearts, I cannot help thinking but that we are on the eve of some very great commotion. This is the Time then for plans of various sorts to be ready, that the Nation may have it in their power to choose one that will prevent the like misfortunes in future, for it is a melancholy thing to see a people after being compelled to throw their

Burdens off their backs till they are laid on again, for want of knowing better.

But we are not without political planners, even where one would hardly expect them. For I overheard a Stable-boy the other day in a great rage telling his companions that nothing would do but a sponge to wipe off at once the whole of the National Debt.

Now this young man is not singular, nay it is the general opinion that nothing less will do us any good. Wherefore when we are about it, and the sponge is yet wet, let us make a clean board, and wipe off the Landed score also. For surely we are not bound in conscience to continue in the payment of Rents for our own Lands, any more than to pay interest for Debts which we never contracted.

It is certainly full time that Mankind were come to a clear understanding about establishing their own happiness. Temporising measures will no longer answer any purpose, but of continuing Anarchy. Mixture of Right and Wrong, and of Liberty and Slavery, did never give long content, and at this enlightened period, will less do so that ever. So that Revolutions will now never cease, or rather the Nations will be in a continual state of Revolution, till perfect Truth and Right be established. Then let us lay aside all sinister and bye views, let us open our eyes to the search of Truth, and let us read, compare, judge, and determine. And when we have happily found the plan that we are convinced will restore Society to its Natural State, let us embrace it with singleness of heart, and propagate the knowledge thereof among our Fellow-creatures with the zeal of Apostles, both "in Season and out of Season".

The public opinion will soon become one on a plain interesting Truth if properly and diligently represented to them. Then in consequence of such laudable diligence we may soon expect to see the people arise as one man, and peacably retake possession of their long lost Rights.

You see Citizen, we have arrived at a very serious crisis. The question is no longer of a lukewarm complexion, or bare curious investigation for vain Men to show their abilities in debating upon, we must now study for Life or Death. The question I say is no longer about which form of Government is most favourable to Liberty, as simply heretofore considered, but which System of Society is most favourable to existence, and capable of delivering us from the deadly mischiefs of great accumulations of wealth, which enable a few rich unfeeling Monsters, to starve whole Nations in spite of all the fruitful Seasons God Almighty can send.

I remain, yours, etc.

Footnotes

1. Thus Gentlemen the very motto as well as Title seems to convey a sufficient Apology.
2. Gentlemen if the Rich according to their own Confession be so debilitated by faring sumptuously and living indolently every Day as to be deprived of "that Health, Strength, or Ability to endure Hardness which the laborious Class enjoy", it must be a charitable attempt to deliver them as well as the Indigent from their respective Misery by abolishing the Causes.
3. The remainder of this letter was the Indictment, and is therefore distinguished by three turned commas.
4. This Letter and Letter 4, were not read to the Jury because the subjects of them, were not adverted to in the Indictment.
5. It is impossible gentlemen for a Poor Man to enjoy equal Rights in Society with Men of overgrown consolidated Estates. There was at Newcastle where I was born a contest (in the days of my youth) between the Magistrates and the Freemen about the Disposal of the Rents of a part of the Town — Moor or Common, which was to be let out in farm for the sake of Improving the Soil. The Magistrates and Common-Council said they would have the Rents, and the Burgesses said the Land was theirs, and therefore the Rents were theirs also, and should be at their disposal. It was tried at the Assizes and the Burgesses gained the Day.

    Now I took a Lesson from this affair which I shall never forget. And I conclude from thence as well as from all that I have ever heard, seen, or read, that the overbearing power of Great Men, by their Revenues, and the power of Samson by his hair are strikingly similar and show such Men to be dangerous companions in Society till they be scalped of their Hair, or Revenues. For it is plain that if the Lords of the Philistines had scalped Samson instead of only shaving him, they might have saved both their Lives and their Temple.
6. Gentlemen I wonder how I came to stumble upon Royalty here, for it is what I am in no wise addicted to, as the Attorney General is very well acquainted with, by means of his Spies. Therefore it ought to be looked on as a mere Inadvertence and which naturally presented itself to the Mind with Nebuchadnezzar. I never conceived Royalty to be entitled to my notice in this business. For if the Land be held by the people in the manner I propose, it is impossible for the Executive Administrators, under whatever denomination, to make any Inroads into the prerogatives of the Public. Wherefore the Titles of King, Consul President, etc., are quite indifferent to me. We know that Kings existed in Sparta for many Centuries, in company with Iron Money and small divisions of Lands. Therefore let not Royalty despair.

7. Remember Gentlemen this affair of the Fleets is now a historical Fact liable to be alluded to by the whole World, and also by Posterity.
8. This is bold reasoning Gentlemen. But who is using it? — And for what purpose? Why it is a Legislator advocating the cause of the whole Human Race, whether now living, or that ever shall live to the end of time. And surely it would not become a person engaged in so august a Cause to be slavishly intimidated, and write as if trembling for fear of paltry consequences.

   But notwithstanding this becoming boldness here is no Tocsin sounded as a signal for massacre no war-whoop for an ignorant Rabble to turn out to burn and destroy. No such thing: It is the irresistible force of Reason, addressed to the thinking part of Mankind, and showing by fair Inference that Men may attain their rights by unanimity, and not otherwise, Therefore what I advance will rather operate as a check to inconsiderate and premature Ardour. For I labour all along to show that Men cannot have their Rights by piecemeal, nor my system by any imperfect Approaches, and that the nearer they seem to come to it by partial Improvements they are only the more unlikely to adopt it, and therefore they must think of having it all at once, or not at all. Thus you see my Labours tend not in the least to Anarchy or Confusion, but the most universal Unanimity.

   For pray Gentlemen who can suppose a few Parishioners to become so wise and so well instructed in their Rights, as to think of adopting my Constitution, without supposing the whole Nation equal so; nay, one may say the whole World? For in these Days, by means of Printing all Nations as well as Individuals and Parishes, learn everything of a General Tendency at the same time. And, then again, who could suppose that only a few Parishes would be so fool-hardy, as to set up a New System, so contrary to former Prejudices and Interests without well knowing that the whole Nation were ripe and ready to join them? And when such a Time comes, no human opposition will avail.

   So you see Gentlemen there is nothing in all this tending to Disorganisation, but the contrary: Here is too much Reason and Justice, too much Order and Solidity for Anarchy, or lovers of Anarchy.
9. This distinguished piece was also in the Indictment.
10. Gentlemen, I can hardly help being diverted at all seeing this Sylvan Joke, Twenty-four years old, made a part of a serious Indictment at this distance of time. It seems as if paying my sagacity a very high Compliment; but at the same time is a pointed Libel on the Abilities and spirit of the whole Nation, as if none beside were qualified to draw such alarming Conclusions and Resolutions, from the Privation of their Rights unless I put them up to it. This shows what strange Metamorphosises are likely to take place in a Man's writings when the spirit of Inuendo begins to move on their surface. I think I need say no more on this ridiculous subject, but take care how I joke for the future, especially in a time of War, and Endeavour henceforth to be dull, yet stupidly dull, as the only means of safety. From such Cowardly Indictments good Lord deliver us!
11. Gentlemen this is not filling the hungry with good things and sending the Rich empty away.
12. In those days even bad as they were, it seems engrossing of land was not arrived at the sublime perfection it has attained to in modern days. There were still, notwithstanding the wickedness of the times, Wildernesses and Commons unclaimed by Lords of Manors. It was therefore possible to get out of the reach of those harpies as we see the Rechabites did. But can we do

so now? No. Pitch our Tents where we will, some or other Lord of the Manor will interrupt us. And would the Rechabites come here, and dare to follow their Father's Injunctions, they would soon occupy the conspicuous situation that I now stand in, for daring to set up such Evil Examples.

13. Defence. I suppose Gentlemen the maritime Parishes would as naturally become Boards of Fisheries as the inland Parishes of Agriculture, and thus no natural advantages would be lost. For what the abilities of Individuals, may be unequal to perform, Parishes would be well able to accomplish.

14. Defence. Now this extreme Purity and Disinterestedness of the scheme, having been the reason why it has not all these Six and Twenty years been able to create a powerful party, the Government, and the Rich had no occasion to be alarmed at it, and accordingly were not. But this I know, it has an odd appearance, after Twenty Six years, Forbearance to put a Man in danger of a Prison for such odd opinions. It did something like Parricide.

The Constitution of Spensonia (1803)

Declaration

The Spensonian People convinced that forgetfulness and contempt for the natural Rights of Man, are the only cause of the Crimes and Misfortunes of the World, have resolved to expose in a declaration their sacred and inalienable rights, in order that all citizens being always able to compare the Acts of the Government, with the ends of every social Institution, may never suffer themselves to be oppressed and degraded by Tyranny; and that the people may always have before their eyes the basis of their liberty and happiness; the magistrates, the rule of their conduct and duty; and legislators, the object of their mission.

They acknowledge therefore and proclaim in the presence of the Supreme Being, the following declaration of the Rights of Man and Citizens:

1. The end of Society is common happiness. Government is instituted to secure to man the enjoyment of his natural and impresceptible rights.
2. These rights are Equality, Liberty, Safety, and Property, natural and acquired.
3. All human beings are equal by nature and before the law, and have a continual and inalienable property in the Earth, and its natural productions.
4. The law is the free and solemn expression of the general will. It ought to be the same for all, whether it protects or punishes. It cannot order but what is just and useful to Society. It cannot forbid but what is hurtful.
5. Social laws, therefore, can never proscribe natural rights.

And every Man, Woman, and Child still retain from the day of their birth, to the day of their death, their primogenial right to the soil of their respective parishes.
6. Thus, after a Parish, out of its Rents, has remitted to the State and County, its legal quota towards their expenses, and provided for defraying its own proper contingencies, the remainder of the Rents is the indisputable joint property of all the Men, Women, and Children having settlement in the parish, and ought to be equally divided among them.
7. All male Citizens are equally admissible to public employments. Free people know no other motives of preference in their Elections than virtue and Talents.
8. Liberty is that power which belongs to a Man of doing everything that does not hurt the right of another. Its principle is nature: Its rule justice: Its protection, the law, and its moral limits are defined by this maxim: "Do not to another what you would not wish done unto yourself".
9. The right of manifesting one's thoughts and opinions either by the press or in any other manner: the right of assembling peaceably, and the free exercise of religious worship cannot be forbidden. The necessity of announcing these rights supposes either the presence or the recent remembrance of despotism.
10. Whatever is not forbidden by the law, cannot be prevented. No one can be forced to do that which the law does not order.
11. Safety consists in the protection granted by Society to each Citizen for the preservation of his person, his rights and his property.
12. The law avenges public and individual liberty of the abuses committed against them by power.
13. No person can be accused, arrested, or confined but in cases determined by the law, and according to the form which it prescribes. Every Citizen summoned or seized by the authority of the law ought immediately to obey, he renders himself culpable by resistance.
14. Every act exercised against a Man to which the cases in

the law do not apply, and in which its forms are not observed, is arbitrary and tyrannical. Respect for the laws forbid him to submit to such acts; and if attempts are made to execute them by violence he has a right to repel force by force.
15. Those who shall solicit, dispatch, sign, execute, or cause to be executed arbitrary acts are culpable and ought to be punished.
16. Every Man being supposed innocent until he has been declared guilty, if it is judged indispensable to arrest him all severity not necessary to secure his person ought to be strictly repressed by the law.
17. No one ought to be tried and punished until he has been legally summoned, and in virtue of a law published previous to the commission of the crime. A law which should punish crimes committed before it existed would be tyrannical. The retroactive effect given to a law would be a crime.
18. The law ought not to decree any punishments but such as are strictly and evidently necessary. Punishments ought to be proportioned to the crime, and useful to Society.
19. The right of property is that which belongs to every Citizen to enjoy and dispose of according to his pleasure, his property, revenues, labour, and industry. Here his property in land is excepted, which being inseparably incorporated with that of his fellow Parishioners is inalienable.
20. No kind of labour, culture, or commerce can be forbidden to the industrious citizen.
21. Every man may engage his services and his time, but he cannot sell himself; his person is not alienable property. The law does not acknowledge servitude; there can exist only an engagement of care and gratitude between the man who labours and the man who employs him.
22. No one can be deprived of the smallest portion of his property without his consent, except when the public necessity, legally ascertained, evidently require it, and on condition of a just and previous indemnification.

23. No public revenue can be established but for general ability, and to relieve the public wants. Every Citizen has a right to concur in the establishment of such revenue; to watch over the use made of it, and to call for a statement of expenditure.
24. Public aids are a sacred debt. The Society is obliged to provide for the subsistence of the unfortunate, either by procuring them work, or by securing the means of existence to those who are unable to labour.
25. Instruction is the want of all, and the Society ought to favour with all its power the progress of the public reason; and to place Instruction, within the reach of every Citizen.
26. The social guarantee consists in the actions of all to secure to each the enjoyment and preservation of his Rights. This guarantee rests on the national Sovereignty.
27. The Social Guarantee cannot exist if the limits of public functions are not clearly determined by the law, and if the responsibility of all public functionaries is not secured.
28. The Sovereignty resides in the people; it is one and indivisible, imprescriptable and inalienable.
29. No proportion of the people can exercise the power of the whole; but each section of the sovereign assembled ought to enjoy the right of expressing its will in perfect liberty. Every individual who arrogates to himself the Sovereignty, or who usurps the exercise of it, ought to be put to death by freemen.
30. A people have always the right of revising, amending, and changing their constitution. One Generation cannot subject to its law future generations.
31. Every Citizen has an equal right of concurring in the formation of the law and in the nomination of his mandatores or agents.
32. Public Functions cannot be considered as distinctions or rewards, but as duties.
33. Crimes committed by the mandatores of the people and their agents ought never to remain unpunished. No one has a right to pretend to be more inviolable than other

Citizens.
34. The right of presenting petitions to the depositories of Public Authority belongs to every individual. The exercise of this right cannot in any case be forbidden, suspended, or limited.
35. Resistance to oppression is the consequence of the other rights of man.
36. Oppression is exercised against the social body, when even one of its members is oppressed. Oppression is exercised against each member when the social body is oppressed.
37. When the Government violates the rights of the people, Insurrection becomes to the people, and to every portion of the people, the most sacred and the most indispensible of duties.

OF THE COMMONWEALTH
1. The Spensonian Commonwealth is one and indivisible.

OF THE DISTRIBUTION OF THE PEOPLE
2. The Spensonian people are distributed for the exercise of its sovereignty and for the management of its landed property into parishes.
3. It is distributed for administration and for justice into counties and parishes.

OF THE STATE OF CITIZENS
4. Every Man or Woman born, or otherwise having acquired a settlement in a parish of Spensonia and of the age of twenty-one years complete; is admitted to the exercise of the rights of a Spensonian Citizen, as far as their sex will allow.
5. Female Citizens have the same right of suffrage in their respective parishes as the Men: because they have equal property in the country, and are equally subject to the laws, and, indeed, they are in every respect, as well on their own account as on account of their children, as deeply interested in every public transaction. But in consideration of the delicacy of their sex, they are

exempted from, and are ineligible to, all public employments.

6. Every Man, Woman, and Child, whether born in wedlock or not (for nature and justice know nothing of illegitimacy), is entitled quarterly to an equal share of the rents of the parish where they have settlement. But the public aids to the State, and the County, must first be deducted, and the expenses of the parish provided for.
7. The settlement of every man whether native or foreigner is in that parish wherein he last dwelt a full year.
8. The Settlement of every Woman when married and living with her husband is in her husband's parish.
9. The settlement of every Widow or unmarried Woman, or Woman separated from her husband is in the parish wherein she last dwelt a full year.
10. The settlement of Children while living with their Father, is in his parish — while living with their Mother only, in hers: and if Orphans or deserted their settlement is in the parish where they became so.
11. No person can receive dividends, or have a vote in two Parishes at the same time.
12. A child, though born in the last hour of the quarter, and a person dying in the first hour of the quarter, shall nevertheless each of them be entitled to their quarterly dividends. Because such occasions are expensive, and the parish must lean to the generous side.
13. The exercise of the rights of a citizen with respect to voting, or public employments, is suspended by the state of accusation, and by condemnation to punishments infamous or afflictive, till recapitation; but his right to a share of the parish revenues, as a human being, can never be annulled but by death or banishment.

OF THE SOVEREIGNTY OF THE PEOPLE

14. The Sovereign people is the universality of Spensonian citizens.
15. It nominates directly its deputies.
16. It deligates to Electors, the choice of administrators, of

public arbitrators, or Criminal Judges, and Judges of appeal.
17. It deliberates on the Laws.

OF THE PARISHES

18. The land with its natural appurtenances, (according to the law of nature) is the common estate of the inhabitants; a parish is therefore a compact portion of the Country, designedly not too large that it may the more easily be managed by the inhabitants with respect to its revenues and police.
19. A parish can levy no tolls or assessments, but the rents of its territory.
20. Its police appertains to it.
21. It nominates its own officers.
22. It supports a public school.
23. Farmers and such as are able to build and repair their own houses, must have leases of twenty-one years, but no longer, that the most desirable situations may not be always engrossed in the same hands, and that Farms and other Tenements may now and then find their value in order that the Parish Revenue receive no damage, by places being let for less than they will bring.
24. For the more effectual preservation of justice in this business, all considerable Farms and Tenements, must at the Expiration Lease be let by public auction, after due Advertisement in the Public Prints.
25. Every Lease-holder must build according to the regulations laid down by the Parish for the sake of order and duration.
26. They must also leave their Buildings, Fixtures, Fences, etc., at the end of their Leases in good tenantable repair and condition, and their lands in good tilth becoming the public spirit of Spensonia.
27. No deputy Landlords are allowed. Therefore no lease-holder can parcel out his houses or lands to sub-tenants. All unfurnished lodgings or parcels of land can only be let by the parish.
28. Nevertheless an innkeeper or private person may oc-

casionally accommodate strangers or others, with lodging in their own furnished apartments, and their cattle with pasturage, etc.
29. And a settlement may be gained by thus residing a great part, or even the whole of the year in the parish in such furnished lodgings.
30. Strangers from abroad, or Spensonians from other parishes, who may become necessitous through sickness or otherwise before they have gained a settlement, must be supported by the parish in which they then sojourn. But such poor being accounted the poor of the nation at large the parishes before they send off their quarterly poundage to the state, shall deduct therefrom the expenses they have been at in supporting such poor strangers.
31. Parishes in Towns, must always keep a sufficiency of small and convenient apartments in good repair for the accommodation of Labourers, Journeymen Mechanics, Widows and others who desire and require but little room. These shall be let by the quarter at equitable rents.
32. Country Parishes shall have a sufficiency of cottages or small and convenient dwellings with little parcels of land adjoining for gardens, etc., to accommodate Labourers in Husbandry, Smiths, Cartwrights and other Tradesmen and people wishing to live in the Country. These to be let by the year at equitable rents.
33. If a Competition arise about one of these small Tenements in Town or Country on account of its more than common desirable situation, etc., it shall be let by auction, and a lease granted. This will prevent murmuring, and also the Tenements from being let under value to the detriment of the parish.
34. If any parish in town or country should become so full of inhabitants as to have all its small tenements occupied, and yet more should be wanted, then it shall divide the first large sort of tenement that becomes vacant by the expiration of its lease into such small tenements, that the free course of population be not

impeded.

35. It shall not be deemed unconstitutional to hold more tenements or leases than one, and even in sundry parishes — because a person's health or business may require him to occupy Tenements in different situations at the same time; as, for instance, in both town and country: — or he may wish to secure the possession of some desirable tenement, that is to let before the lease of the place he holds at present expires.
36. In such cases as this where settlements in more parishes than one are acquired, such pluralist shall yet vote and receive dividends but in one parish, which parish shall be that which he makes choice of. This restriction is necessary to check the natural ambition and rapacity of the rich.
37. A lease-holder may give up his lease when he pleases to the parish, or sell it for the remainder of the term it has to run to another person.
38. The parishes shall receive rent quarterly from the state, and the county, for the ground which they may have occasion respectively to occupy by their buildings, at a fair valuation: — as State Palaces, Castles, Fortifications, Magazines, Dockyards, etc., County Halls, Hospitals, Jails, etc.
39. Every parish shall constantly have a quantity of corn laid up in store, in proportion to its population, as a reserve against famine or scarcity from bad seasons: and by selling off yearly the oldest, and replacing the quantity with new corn, have it always in the best state.
40. To prevent the parishes from imbibing hereby a spirit of speculation in corn, to the detriment of the country at large, the law will properly regulate this business.
41. The parishes shall take care, that all the hedges do consist only of standard and low spreading grafted Fruit Trees, Shrubs valued for their Fruits and Flowers, and Trees indispensably necessary for their wood, instead of Thorns, Briars, and Brambles. The Spensonians, being the Landlords, are so much interested in the welfare of the Husbandman, and so public-spirited from their

childhood that they will never break his fences or trespass on his grounds, and therefore he may safely cultivate the most inviting vegetables close to the highway side. He has only cattle to guard against.
42. Hunting is forbidden, being inadmissible in a country so highly cultivated, because of the unavoidable destruction it must make. The game, therefore, is considered as going with the ground, and as the sole property of the occupier, who alone may kill all he finds on his premises.
43. All rents shall be brought to the parish counting-house by Twelve o'clock on quarter-day that the books may then be closed. On quarter-day the rents shall be paid to the Parish Officers at their Counting House.
44. During the ensuing week, the parish accounts shall be made up, and after setting aside the poundages due to the state and the county, and settling all internal parochial business, and finding how much of the rent remains to be returned to the people, the accounts shall be minutely printed, including the names of all the Men, Women, and Children, who are entitled to dividends as parishioners, distinguishing those of age to vote by an asterisk.
45. The Eighth day after quarter-day, and the two following (which are always days of festivity) the people come for their dividends, which together with copies of the parish accounts is given to the heads of families, according to the number of their respective households, and to single claimants.

OF THE NATIONAL REPRESENTATION

46. The parishes are the sole basis of the national representation.
47. There is one deputy for each parish if the number of parishes in the nation do not exceed one thousand.
48. If above one thousand, then the parishes in each county shall be classed in pairs of adjacent parishes, after first, if there be an odd parish, determining by lot which shall be it, for it will have the privilege of sending a deputy of itself, as if it were a pair.

49. If the parishes in the nation exceed two thousand, the parishes in each county are divided into classes consisting each of three adjacent parishes, after first deciding by lot as above, if there be one or two odd, which they are, and erecting it or them into a class, observing if there be two that they be adjacent. And so in like manner with any number of parishes that the national representation may never exceed one thousand.
50. The election proceeds in every parish of a class on the same day, and after casting up the votes, send a Commissioner for the general casting up, to the place pointed out by the parish.
51. The nomination is made by the absolute majority of individual suffrages.
52. If the casting up does not give an absolute majority, a second vote is proceeded to, and the votes are taken for the two Citizens who had the most voices.
53. In case of equality of voices, the eldest has the preference, either to be on the ballot or elected. In case of equality of age, lot decides.
54. Every male Citizen exercising the rights of Citizens, is eligible through the extent of the Commonwealth.
55. Each deputy belongs to the whole nation.
56. In case of non-acceptance, resignation, forfeiture, or death of a deputy, he is replaced by the parish or parishes, which nominated him.
57. A deputy who has given in his resignation cannot quit his past, but after the admission of his successor.
58. The Spensonian people assemble every year in their parishes on the first of May, for the elections.
59. They proceed whatever be the number of Citizens present, having a right to vote.

OF ELECTORAL ASSEMBLIES

60. The Citizens meet in their parishes, nominate two Electors for the County.
61. The electoral assembles proceed in their elections as the parishes.

OF THE LEGISLATIVE BODY

62. The Legislative Body is one and indivisible and permanent.
63. Its Session is for a year.
64. It meets the first of July.
65. The National Assembly cannot be constituted if it does not consist of one more than the half the deputies.
66. The Deputies cannot be examined, accused or tried at any time for the opinions they have delivered in the legislative body.
67. They may for a criminal act be seized, but a warrant of arrest, or a warrant summoning to appear, cannot be granted against them, unless authorised by the Legislative Body.

HOLDING OF THE SITTINGS OF THE LEGISLATIVE BODY

68. The Sittings of the National Assembly are public.
69. The Minutes of the Sittings are printed.
70. It cannot deliberate if it be not composed of — Members at least.
71. It cannot refuse to hear its members speak in the order which they have demanded to be heard.
72. It deliberates by a majority of the members present.
73. Fifty members have a right to require the appeal nominal.
74. It has the right of censure on the conduct of its members in its bosom.
75. The police appertains to it in the place of its sittings, and in the external circuit which it has determined.

OF THE FUNCTIONS OF THE LEGISLATIVE BODY

76. The Legislative Body, proposes laws and passes decrees.
77. Under the general name of laws are comprehended the acts of the Legislative Body concerning the legislation, civil and criminal; the general administration of the National Revenues, and the ordinary expenses of the Commonwealth; the title, the weight and impression, and the denomination of money; the declaration of war; the public instruction; the public honours to the memory

of great men.

78. Under the particular name of Decrees are included the acts of the Legislative Body concerning the annual establishment of the Land and Sea Forces; the permission or the prohibition of the passage of foreign Troops, through the Spensonian Territory; the introduction of Foreign Naval Forces into the ports of the Commonwealth; the measures of general safety and tranquility; the annual and momentary distribution of public succours and works; the orders for the fabrication of money of every kind; the unforeseen and extraordinary expenses; the measures local and particular to an administration, or any kind of public works; the defence of the territory; the ratification of Treaties; the nomination and the removal of Commanders in Chief of Armies; the prosecution of the responsibility of members of the Council, and the public functionaries; the accusation of persons charged with plots against the general safety of the Commonwealth all changed in the partial distribution of the Spensonian Territory; national recompenses.

OF THE FORMATION OF THE LAW

79. The plans of laws are preceded by reports.
80. The Discussion cannot be opened, and the law cannot be provisionally resolved upon till fifteen days after the report.
81. The plan is printed and sent to all the parishes of the Commonwealth, under this title "Law Proposed".
82. Forty days after the sending of the Law proposed, if in more than one half of the Counties, the tenth of the Parishes have not objected to it, the plan is accepted and becomes Law.
83. If there be an objection the Legislative Body convokes the parishes.

OF THE ENTITLING OF LAWS AND DECREES

84. Laws, Decrees, Judgments, and all Public Acts are entitled: "In the Name of the Spensonian People, the year of the Spensonian Commonwealth".

OF THE EXECUTIVE COUNCIL

85. There is one Executive Council composed of Twenty-four Members.
86. The Electoral Assembly of each county nominates One Candidate, if the number of Counties in the nation exceeds Twenty: Four, but if under then each County nominates Two. The Legislative Body chooses the members of the Council from the general list.
87. One half of it is renewed by each Legislature in the last month of the Session.
88. The Council is charged with the direction and superintendence of the General Administration. It cannot act but in Execution of the Laws, and Decrees of the Legislative Body.
89. It nominates not of its own body, the agents in chief of the general administration of the Commonwealth.
90. The Legislative Body determines the number and functions of these Agents.
91. These Agents do not form a Council. They are separated without any intermediate correspondence between them; they exercise no personal authority.
92. The Council nominates not of its own body, the external agents of the Commonwealth.
93. It negotiates Treaties.
94. The members of the Council in case of malversation are accused by the Legislative Body.
95. The Council is responsible for the non-execution of laws, and decrees, and for abuses which it does not denounce.
96. It recalls and replaces the Agents in its nomination.
97. It is bound to denounce them if there be occasion before the Judicial Authorities.

OF THE CONNEXION OF THE EXECUTIVE COUNCIL WITH THE LEGISLATIVE BODY

98. The Executive Council resides near the Legislative Body. It has admittance and a separate seat in the place of sittings.
99. It is heard as often as it has an account to give.

100. The Legislative Body calls it into the place of its Sittings in whole or in part when it thinks fit.

THE ADMINISTRATIVE AND COUNTY BODIES
101. There is a central administration in each County.
102. The Officers and Administrators are nominated by the electoral assemblies of the County.
103. The administrations are renewed one half every year.
104. The Administrators and County Officers have no character of representation; they cannot in any case modify the Acts of the Legislative Body, or suspend the execution of them.
105. The Legislative Body determines the functions of the County Officers and Administrators, the rules of their subordination, and the penalties they may incur.
106. The Sittings of Administrations are public.
107. The Electoral Assemblies assess their parishes by a pound rate, quarterly, towards defraying the public expenses of the County, as in building and repairing the County Edifices, such as Halls, Hospitals, Jails, Bridges, and in making and repairing Harbours, Roads, etc.
108. The accounts of the County are settled annually, and, being as minutely printed as to give satisfaction, are sent to the Parishes.

OF CIVIL JUSTICE
109. The code of Civil and Criminal Laws, is uniform for all the Commonwealth.
110. No infringement can be made of the right which Citizens have, to cause their differences to be pronounced upon by Arbitrators of their choice.
111. The decision of these arbitrators is final if the Citizens have not reserved the right of objecting to them.
112. There are Justices of the Peace elected by the Citizens in the parishes.
113. They conciliate and judge without expense.
114. There are public arbitrators elected by the Electoral Assemblies.
115. Their number and their circuits are fixed by the Legis-

lative Body.
116. They take cognizance of disputes which have not been finally determined by the private arbitrations of the Justices of the Peace.
117. They deliberate in public, they give their opinions aloud; they pronounce in the last resort on verbal defences or simple memorials without Procedures, and without expense; they assign the reasons of their decision.
118. The Justices of the Peace and the public arbitrators are elected every year.

OF CRIMINAL JUSTICE

119. In Criminal cases no Citizen can be tried but by an examination received by a Jury, or decreed by the Legislative Body, the accused have counsel chosen by themselves or nominated officially; the process is public; the fact and the intention are declared by a Jury of Judgement; the punishment is applied by a Criminal Tribunal.
120. Criminal Judges are elected every year by the Electoral Assemblies.

OF THE TRIBUNAL OF APPEAL

121. There is one Tribunal of Appeal for all the Commonwealth.
122. This Tribunal does not take cognisance of the merits of the case: it pronounces on the violation of forms and an express contravention of the Law.
123. The members of the Tribunal are nominated every year by the Electoral Assembly.

OF THE NATIONAL TREASURY

124. The National Treasury is the central point of the receipts and expenses of the Commonwealth.
125. It is supplied by an assessment raised quarterly of — in the pound, on the rents of the parishes by the Legislative Body.
126. This assessment being sufficient for all national purposes, and being sent up by the parishes every quarter without

expenses, renders revenues, laws and officers unnecessary.
127. The affairs of the Treasury are administered by accountable agents, nominated by the Executive Council.
128. These agents are superintended by Commissioners nominated by the Legislative Body, not of its own members, and responsible for abuses which they do not denounce.

OF ACCOUNTABILITY

129. The accounts of the agents of the national treasure, and of the administrators of the public money are given in annually to responsible Commissioners nominated by the Executive Council.
130. These verifications are superintended by Commissioners in the nomination of the Legislative Body, not of its own members, and responsible for errors, and abuses which they do not denounce; the Legislative Body passes the accounts.
131. The National Accounts are printed yearly sufficiently minute to give satisfaction, and sent to the parishes.

OF THE FORCES OF THE COMMONWEALTH

132. The General Forces of the Commonwealth are composed of the whole people.
133. The Commonwealth maintains in its pay, even in times of peace, an armed force by sea and land.
134. All the Spensonians are soldiers; they are all exercised in the use of Arms.
135. There is no Generalissimo.
136. Difference of ranks, their distinctive marks, and subordination subsist only with relation to service, and during its continuance.
137. The public force employed for maintaining order and peace in the interior, does not act but on the requisition in writing of the Constituted Authorities.
138. The public force employed against enemies from without acts under the order of the Executive Council.
139. No armed bodies can deliberate.

OF THE REVISION OF THE CONSTITUTION

140. If in one more than half of the Counties, the tenth of the parishes of each regularly assembled demand the revision of the constitutional act or the change of some of its articles, the legislative body is bound to convoke all the parishes of the Commonwealth, to know if there be ground for a revision of the Constitution.
141. The assembly of revision is formed by two members from each County.
142. The assembly of revision exercises no function of legislation or of Government; it confines itself to the revision of the Constitutional Laws.
143. All the authorities continue the exercise of their functions, till the change proposed in the assembly of revision, shall have been accepted by the people, and till the new Authorities shall have been put in motion.
144. The assembly of revision addresses immediately to the parishes, the plan of reform which it has agreed upon. It is dissolved as soon as its plan has been addressed.

OF THE CORRESPONDENCE OF THE SPENSONIAN COMMONWEALTH, WITH OTHER NATIONS

145. The Spensonian people is the friend and natural ally of every free people.
146. It does not interfere in the Government of other Nations. It does not suffer other nations to interfere in its own.
147. It gives an asylum to Foreigners banished from their Country for the cause of liberty; it refuses it to Tyrants.
148. It does not make peace with an enemy that occupies its territory.

OF THE GUARANTEE OF RIGHTS

149. The Constitution guarantees to all the Spensonians, Equality, Liberty, Safety, Property, parochial and private, the free exercise of worship, a common instruction, public succours; the indefinite liberty of the Press, the right of petition, the right of meeting in popular Societies, the enjoyment of all the Rights of Man.
150. The Spensonian Commonwealth honours Loyalty,

courage, filial piety, misfortune. It puts the deposit of its Constitution under the guard of all virtues.

151. The declaration of rights, and the Constitutional Act are engraven on tables in the bosom of the Legislative Body and in the public places.

OF COLONISATION

152. Spensonia disclaims all financial benefits from foreign Provinces, Dominions, or Colonies.
153. Yet because the unparalleled encouragement to marriage, and of the influx of Foreigners, must inevitably so increase the number of inhabitants under this Constitution, that Colonies enjoying the same blessings must be established as inviting offings for the redundance of population on the Mother Country to flow to.
154. All the Colonies (therefore) that now belong to Spensonia, or shall be hereafter established by her, are declared independent states, as soon as they adopt and put in practice similar Constitutions. They shall then be considered as in the most intimate state of alliance, and entitled to all the protection the Mother Country can afford.
155. To promote cleanliness and refresh the spirit of men and labouring animals, the weeks in Spensonia are but five days each; every fifth day being a day or Sabbath of Rest. Thus will the fourth day of the week be always a market day and a pay day for labourers.

THOMAS SPENCE

EPILOGUE

What pity Friends that we should be,
So much deprived of Liberty!
Indictments one upon another
Continually do us bother.
How carefully we're forced to seek
For words before we dare to speak!
But let what will upon me come,
I scorn to close my work quite dumb.
'And though my book's in queer lingo,
I will it send to St. Domingo:
To the Republic of the Incas,
For an example how to frame Laws.
For who can tell but the Millennium
May take its rise from my poor Cranium?
And who knows but it God may please
It should come by the West Indies?
No harm I mean by this reflection;
And thus I end my application.
                                    T.S.

III
Bibliography
of
Thomas Spence

THOMAS SPENCE

The Grand Repository of the English Language containing besides the excellencies of all other dictionaries and grammars of the English tongue, the peculiarity of having the most proper and agreeable pronunciation of the alphabetic words denoted in the most intelligible manner by a new alphabet, with a copper-plate exhibiting the new alphabet both in writing and printing characters, intended for the use of everyone whether native or foreigner that would acquire a complete knowledge of the English language with the least waste of time and expense but especially for those who are but indifferent readers not having been taught to pronounce properly (Newcastle, 1775).

The Real Reading made Easy or foreigners' and grown-up persons' pleasing introduction to reading English whereby all persons, of whatever age or nature, may soon be taught with ease and pleasure to read the English Language (Newcastle, 1782).

A Supplement to the History of Robinson Crusoe, Being the History of Crusonia, or Robinson Crusoe's Island, Down to the present Time. Copied from a letter sent by Mr Wishit, Captain of the Good-Intent, to an intelligent Friend in England, after being in a storm in May, 1781 driven out of his course to the said Island. Published by the said Gentleman, for the agreeable perusal of Robinson Crusoe's Friends of all sizes (Newcastle, 1782).

The Case of Thomas Spence, Bookseller, the Corner of Chancery Lane, London, who was committed to Clerkenwell Prison on Monday the 10th of December 1792 for Selling the Second part of Paine's "Rights of Man", and a bill of indictment found against him to which is added an extract of a letter from His Grace the Duke of Richmond to the Chairman of the Committee of the County of Sussex convened at Jewes, Jan. 18th 1783 for the purpose of presenting a petition to the House of Commons to take into consideration the unequal state of representation in Parliament, etc. (London, 1792).

The Rights of Man. A Political Song (London, 1793).

Burke's Address to the Swinish Multitude (London, 1793).

The Rights of Man, as exhibited in a Lecture, Read at the Philosophical Society, in Newcastle, to which is now first added, An Interesting Conversation, Between a Gentleman and the Author, on the Subject of his Scheme. With the Queries sent by the Rev Mr J. Murray, to the Society in Defence of the Same. And a Song of Triumph for the People, on the Recovery of their long lost Rights (London, 1793).

Pigs' Meat; or Lessons for the Swinish Multitude. Published in Weekly Penny Numbers, Collected by the Poor Man's Advocate (an old Veteran in the Cause of Freedom) in the Course of his Reading for more than Twenty Years. Intended to promote among the Labouring Part of Mankind proper Ideas of their Situation, of their Importance, and of their Rights. And to Convince them that their forlorn Condition has not been entirely overlooked and forgotten, nor their just cause unpleaded, neither by their Maker nor by the best and most enlightened Men in all Ages (3 vols; London, 1793-1795).

The End of Oppression; Being a Dialogue Between an Old Mechanic and a Young One. Concerning the Establishment of the Rights of Man (London, 1795).

Spence's Recantation of the End of Oppression London, 1795).

A Letter from Ralph Hodge, to his cousin Thomas Bull (London, 1795).

The Coin Collector's Companion being a descriptive alphabetical list of the modern provincial and other copper coins, No.8, Little Turnstile, High Holborn, 1795 (London, 1795).

The Meridian Sun of Liberty; or, The Whole Rights of Man Displayed and most Accurately Defined, in a Lecture read at the Philosophical Society in Newcastle, on the 8th of November, 1775, for printing of which the Society did the Author the honour to expel him. To which is now first prefixed, by way of Preface, a most important Dialogue between the Citizen Reader and the Author (London, 1796).

The Reign of Felicity being a plan for civilizing the Indians of North America without infringing on their national or individual independence, in a coffee house dialogue between a courtier, an esquire, a clergyman and a farmer (London, 1796).

A Fragment of Ancien Prophecy relating as some think to the present Revolutions (being the fourth part of the "End of Oppression") and 2 odes by P Pinder (London, 1796).

The Rights of Infants; or, the Imprescriptable Right of Mothers to such a Share of the Elements as is sufficient to enable them to suckle and bring up their young. In a Dialogue between the Aristocracy and a Mother of Children. To which are added, by way of Preface and Appendix, Strictures on Paine's Agrarian Justice (London, 1797).

The Constitution of a Perfect Commonwealth amended and rendered entirely conformable to the whole rights of man. Finis coronat opus the second edition with a preface how to study politics by T. Spence, author and publisher of that best repository of sound and standard politics entitled "Pigs' Meat", and of several traits on the imprescriptible Rights of Mankind (London, 1798).

The Restorer of Society, To Its Natural State, In A Series of letters to a Fellow Citizen. With a Preface, containing the objections of a Gentleman who perused the Manuscript, and the Answers by the Author (London, 1801).

The Important Trial of Thomas Spence for a political pamphlet entitled *The Restorer of Society to its Natural State, on May 27th, 1801, at Westminster Hall, before Lord Kenyon and a special jury* (London, 1803).

The Constitution of Spensonia, A Country in Fairy-land, Situated between Utopia and Oceana Brought from thence by Captain Swallow (London, 1803).

The Giant-Killer, or Anti-Landlord (London, 1814).

Spence's Songs (3 parts; London, n.d.).

Something to the Purpose. A receipt to make a millenium or happy world. Being extracts from the Constitution of Spensonia (London, n.d.).

The Jubilee Hymn. To be sung an hundred Years hence, or sooner (London, n.d.).

A New and Infallible Way to Make Trade (London, n.d.).

A Suitable Companion to Spence's Songs: A Fable (London, n.d.).

The Pronouncing and Foreigners' Bible, containing the old and New Testament being, not only the properest book for establishing a uniform and permanent manner of speaking, the sonorous, harmonious and agreeable English and also infinitely preferable to any introductory book hitherto contrived for teaching children or grown persons upon whose mother-tongue it is, but is likewise peculiarly calculated to render English universal, for by this book foreigners of any country may be taught to read English much easier than their own respective languages; recommended as the most proper book for Sunday Schools, by T. Spence, Teacher of English, London (London, n.d.).

Unpublished
"Correspondence with Charles Hall", 1807.
"Of Nobility", n.d.

Chief Sources: British Museum, Main Library and Place Papers, Goldsmith's Library, Newcastle Public Library.